FLIGHT AND FIGHT

At first, even under a double load, the Ovaro's superior speed and endurance opened up a slight lead. Soon, however, the attackers began to slowly gain, bullets raining in more accurately. A yellow cloud of dust boiled up behind the pursuers.

"We can't outrun 'em!" Fargo called to his friend. "So let's outgun 'em!"

Buckshot rallied behind him. "Put at 'em, Trailsman!"

Fargo had learned that when escape was impossible, a sudden surprise attack was often the best option. He wheeled the Ovaro and both men shucked out their short guns.

Raising war whoops, revolvers blazing, they charged into the teeth of the attack. A man twisted in his saddle, blood blossoming from his wounded arm. Fargo emptied his wheel, took the reins in his teeth, and popped in his spare cylinder. With his third shot the lead rider slumped in his saddle, his jaw blown half off, then slipped from his mount. . . .

THE
TRAILSMAN
#379

HANGTOWN
HELLCAT

by

Jon Sharpe

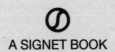

A SIGNET BOOK

SIGNET
Published by the Penguin Group
Penguin Group (USA) Inc., 375 Hudson Street, New York, New York 10014, USA

USA / Canada / UK / Ireland / Australia / New Zealand / India / South Africa / China
Penguin Books Ltd., Registered Offices: 80 Strand, London WC2R 0RL, England
For more information about the Penguin Group visit penguin.com.

First published by Signet, an imprint of New American Library,
a division of Penguin Group (USA) Inc.

First Printing, May 2013

The first chapter of this book previously appeared in *Wyoming Wildcat*, the three
hundred seventy-eighth volume in this series.

 REGISTERED TRADEMARK—MARCA REGISTRADA

ISBN 978-0-451-41750-3

Printed in the United States of America
10 9 8 7 6 5 4 3 2 1

The Trailsman

Beginnings . . . they bend the tree and they mark the man. Skye Fargo was born when he was eighteen. Terror was his midwife, vengeance his first cry. Killing spawned Skye Fargo, ruthless, cold-blooded murder. Out of the acrid smoke of gunpowder still hanging in the air, he rose, cried out a promise never forgotten.

The Trailsman they began to call him all across the West: searcher, scout, hunter, the man who could see where others only looked, his skills for hire but not his soul, the man who lived each day to the fullest, yet trailed each tomorrow. Skye Fargo, the Trailsman, the seeker who could take the wildness of a land and the wanting of a woman and make them his own.

Wyoming (Nebraska Territory), 1861—where a dangerously beautiful woman entices Fargo into an outlaw hellhole where honest men dance on air.

1

"We're in some deep soup, Fargo," said "Big Ed" Creighton, surveying the latest damage to his life's dream. "Back in the rolling grass country we were making up to twelve miles a day. Between twenty-two and twenty-five poles per mile, slick as snot on a saddle horn. But I didn't take the buffalo into account."

Creighton cursed under his breath and knocked the dottle from his pipe on the heel of his boot.

"I'll have to send men back to set the poles again," he said bitterly. "They were inferior wood to begin with, but all we had. Most have been snapped—turned into scratch poles for the blasted bison!"

The tall, lean, wide-shouldered man dressed in buckskins said nothing to this tirade, merely removed his hat to shoo away flies with it. His calm, fathomless lake blue eyes stayed in constant motion, studying the surrounding slopes dotted with stands of juniper and scrub pine. From long habit as a scout, Skye Fargo watched for movement or reflection, not shapes.

"Two days before Independence Day," Creighton mused aloud, his tone almost wistful, "me and Charlie dug the first posthole in Julesburg, Colorado. Even with the nation plunging into war, President Lincoln himself took time to wish us luck. Think of it, Fargo! For the first time telegraphic dispatches will be sent from ocean to ocean."

Fargo did think about it and felt guilt lance into him deep. He glanced up into a storybook perfect Western sky: ragged white parcels of cloud slid across a sky the pure blue color of a gas flame. The flat, endless horizon of eastern Wyoming was behind them, and now the magnificent, ermine-capped peaks of the Rockies—still called the Great Stony Mountains by the old trappers—surrounded them in majestic profusion.

And here's the fiddle-footed Trailsman, Fargo told himself, helping to blight it with a transcontinental telegraph that will only draw in settlements like flies to syrup. But at the time Creighton offered him fifty dollars a month to work as a scout and hunter, Fargo was light in the pockets and out of work.

All that was bad enough. But as Fargo read the obvious signs that Big Ed had missed, the words *pile on the agony* snapped in his mind like burning twigs.

"Buffalo!" Creighton spat out the word like a bad taste. "Fargo, we're already on a mighty tight schedule. My contract allows me a hundred and twenty days to link up with Jim Gamble's crew in Utah. If this keeps up, and we get trapped in a Wyoming winter . . ."

Creighton trailed off, for both men knew damn well what that would mean. Fargo had seen snow pile up so deep, and for so long, in these parts that rabbits suffocated in their burrows. He recalled being caught in a blizzard just north of here that forced him to shelter inside a hollowed-out log for three days.

Stringing this line in late summer was travail enough, too. Mosquitoes all night, flies all day. Sometimes they drove men and beasts into frenzied fits. Trees to provide telegraph poles often had to be freighted great distances, as did the supplies needed to keep a virtual army of workers fed, clothed, and equipped.

And most vexing of all was the serious lack of drinking water. Fargo had spent more time locating water than he had hunting or scouting.

Now came this new trouble—Fargo studied the ground around the downed poles and felt a familiar foreboding. Instinct told him that, soon, lead would fly.

"Well," Creighton said, kicking at one of the broken poles, "wha'd'ya think? I could use the pocket relay and telegraph back to Fort Laramie. Maybe Colonel Langford could send enough soldiers to scatter the herds away from these parts."

Fargo shook his head. "The Laramie garrison has always been undermanned. And now half the troops have been ordered back east. That leaves just enough for force protection at the fort."

Creighton expelled a long, fluming sigh, nodding at the truth of Fargo's words. "Speak the truth and shame the devil. You got any suggestions?"

Fargo glanced at his employer. Big Ed Creighton, the son of penniless Irish immigrants, was a ruddy-complexioned, barrel-chested man in early middle age with a frank, weather-seamed face. He wore a broad-brimmed plainsman's hat, sturdy linsey-woolsey trousers, and calfskin boots. He was the rainmaker for this ambitious project and a damn good man for the job, in Fargo's estimation. He rode every mile of this route before he mapped it out, and now he was working right alongside his men, eating the same food and taking the same risks.

One thing he was not, however, was a good reader of sign.

"Ed," Fargo said, "it's true that great shaggy brought down some poles back in the grassland. And we are sticking mostly to bottomland and valleys lately where you'll sometimes spot herds. But does the ground around us look like it's been torn up by sharp hooves?"

"Why . . ." Creighton surveyed the area around them. "Why, no. In fact, the grass isn't even flattened, is it?"

Fargo watched a skinny yellow coyote slink off through a nearby erosion gully. Clearly the boss did not like the turn this trail was taking.

"Then it must be Indians," Creighton said.

Fargo snorted. "I'd call that idea a bug of the genus hum. Sure, there's been Lakota and Cheyennes watching us like cats on a rat. They don't like what they see, and I don't blame them. But they don't understand what we're up to, and when the red man doesn't understand something he tends to wade in slow. Everything connected to the white man is likely to be bad medicine—they aren't touching those poles. Not yet, anyhow."

Creighton looked like a man who had woken up in the wrong year. The weather grooves in his face deepened when he frowned. "You yourself are always pointing out how the

Indians are notional and unpredictable. Back in western Missouri, the Fox tribe learned how to use stolen crowbars to rip up railroad tracks."

Fargo sighed patiently. "Indian scares" were common because they stirred up settlers. Stirred-up settlers meant more soldiers, and thus, more lucrative contracts to the eastern opportunists supplying them.

"Ed, if it was Indians who tore down these poles, then their horses have iron-shod hooves."

These words struck Creighton like a bolt out of the blue. He hung fire for a few seconds, not understanding. "You're saying white men did this?"

"'Pears so."

"But . . . Fargo, there's nary a settlement anywhere near here. *What* white men?"

"That's got me treed," Fargo admitted. "But there were three of them, and they rode out headed due south. Buckshot left at sunup going after game. He should be back anytime now. We'll pick up that trail and see where it takes us."

"White men," Creighton repeated as the men headed toward the two mounts calmly taking off the grass nearby. "Why would white men go to such trouble to sabotage a telegraph line?"

Fargo forked leather and reined his Ovaro around to the west, pressuring him to a trot with his knees.

"Because," he suggested, "the telegraph is even faster than a posse. There's been strikes against bull trains and mail carriers in this neck of the woods. Even a few kidnappings of stagecoach passengers on the Overland route. Good chance the owlhoot gang behind those crimes don't want that telegraph going through. Back east, the talking wires have put the kibosh on plenty of road agents."

"All that rings right enough," Creighton agreed reluctantly, gigging his blaze-faced sorrel up beside Fargo's black-and-white stallion.

"It does and it doesn't," Fargo hedged, keeping a weather eye out and loosening his 16-shot Henry repeater in its saddle scabbard. "Most outlaws are a lazy tribe with damn poor trailcraft. They like good meals, saloons, and beds with a whore in them. You'll most often find them in towns, not

4

running all over Robin Hood's barn. Like you said, there's no settlements around here."

"Right now," Creighton said, "Jim Gamble and his Pacific crew are racing to beat us to Fort Bridger. Working in those God-forgotten deserts of Nevada and Utah. Black cinder mountains, alkali dust, and warpath Paiutes—until now, I figured we had the easy part."

"You might be building a pimple into a peak," Fargo reminded him despite his own growing sense of unease. "If it's just three outlaws, me and Buckshot will salt their tails. That sort of work is right down our alley."

"You two are just the boys to do it," Creighton agreed. "It's *water* I'm really fretting about. I'll tell you who will soon get rich out west—well diggers and men who build windmills to drive the water. You won't find one in a nickel novel, but one man with a steam drill is worth a shithouse full of gunslingers."

"I respect honest labor, Ed, but to hell with wells and windmills."

Creighton flashed a grin through the dusty patina on his face. "To hell with this magnetic telegraph too, huh?"

Fargo grinned back. "I'm straddling the fence on that one," he admitted. "Couriers and express riders are murdered every day, including some good friends of mine. It's an ill Chinook that doesn't blow *some*body some good, I reckon."

By now the two men had ridden into sight of the main work crew. Under the watchful eye of Taffy Blackford, the Welsh foreman, workers were busy digging postholes, setting and shaping poles, and stringing wire. Other men had scattered out to scavenge wood for poles. A carpenter was at work repairing the broken tongue of a wagon.

"Here comes Buckshot now," Fargo remarked, spotting a rider approaching them on a grulla, an Indian-broke bluish gray mustang also known as a smoky. "Something must be on the spit. He rode out without eating and he's always hungry as a field hand when he gets back. He'd ought to be feeding his face right about now."

Buckshot Brady had been hired at Fargo's insistence. He was an ace Indian tracker and experienced frontiersman who had learned his lore at the side of Kit Carson and Uncle Dick Wootton during the shining times at Taos. He earned his name from carrying a sawed-off double ten in a special-rigged swivel sling on his right hip.

Buckshot loped closer and Fargo saw that his face was grim as an undertaker's.

"Trouble, old son?" Fargo greeted him.

"Skye," Buckshot replied quietly, drawing rein, "I got me a God-fear."

The hair on Fargo's nape instantly stiffened. Buckshot's famous "God-fears" were as reliable as the equinox.

"Ed," Fargo snapped, tugging his brass-framed Henry from its boot, "whistle the men to cover."

"What's—?"

"Now!" Fargo ordered and Creighton reached for the silver whistle on its chain beneath his collar.

Just then, however, a hammering racket of gunfire erupted from the boulder-strewn slope on their left. Fargo watched, his blood icing, as a rope of blood spurted from one side of the carpenter's head and he folded to the ground like an empty gunnysack.

"God-in-whirlwinds!" a shocked Ed Creighton exclaimed.

An eyeblink later, the withering volley of lead shifted to the three men, and Creighton, too, crashed to the ground, trapped under his dying horse.

2

Fargo had no idea how badly Creighton was injured. But with slugs snapping and wind ripping past the Trailsman's ears, it wasn't the time to find out.

Simultaneously, he and Buckshot swung out of the saddle and threw arms around their horses' necks. Both mounts were trained to lie on their sides when wrestled down. Using their horses as bulwarks, they searched for their targets.

Fargo spotted curls of dark gray powder smoke. "That rock nest halfway up the slope!" he shouted to Buckshot.

In moments Fargo's Henry and Buckshot's North & Savage revolving-cylinder rifle were barking furiously. Again and again the lever-action Henry bucked into Fargo's shoulder socket as brass casings flew from the ejector port, glinting in the bright sunlight.

Their fusillade sent up a high-pitched whine as bullets ricocheted through the boulders above them. Soon the firing from the slope tapered off, then ceased completely as the attackers chose discretion over valor and escaped down the back side of the slope. Fargo heard the rataplan of hooves as their horses escaped to the south.

"You hurt bad?" Fargo asked his boss. He and Buckshot heaved mightily on the dead sorrel.

Creighton grunted. "Just trapped my leg. A little more, fellas. A little more . . ."

With another grunt he rolled free and gingerly sat up, feeling his left leg. "Nothing broken. I'll be limping for a few days, but damn it to hell! I paid two hundred dollars for this horse!"

Fargo whistled the Ovaro up and helped hoist Creighton into the saddle.

"I counted three shooters," Buckshot told Fargo as they started forward, leading their horses.

"Same here," Fargo said. "Likely the same three who brought down the poles last night."

"The war kettle is on the fire," Buckshot said grimly, watching a knot of men gather around the murdered carpenter. "That's Dan Appling they knocked out from under his hat."

"A damn good man," Creighton added from the saddle. "With a wife back in Ohio."

"And two pups on the rug," Buckshot said. "Dan showed me a tintype of his family. Let's me and you get horsed, Skye, and drill some lead into them three sons-a-bitches' livers."

Fargo glanced at his fellow hunter and scout. Buckshot was Choctaw on his mother's side and had a hawk nose and no facial hair. His long silver mane was tied off in back with a rawhide whang under a snap-brim hat.

"Bad idea," Fargo said. "Be damn easy to dry-gulch riders in this country. We'll track them down, right enough, and put paid to this account. But let them get a day ahead of us. We can't let them spot our hand before we play it."

Buckshot had ridden into his share of traps, and now he nodded reluctantly. "That shines. Revenge is a dish best served cold, huh?"

"Anybody else hit?" Creighton demanded as the trio joined the main gather.

"Two men wounded," Taffy Blackford replied. "Steve Mumford and Ron Shoemaker. They'll be all right if their wounds don't mortify."

Fargo took a quick look at the wounded men.

"The bullet passed clean through Steve's forearm," he announced. "Just flush it good with carbolic and wrap it. Ron's caught a slug in the meat of his thigh, and I recommend leaving the bullet in him—it's not close to anything dangerous. Flush the hole good and then cram it with beef tallow to stem the bleeding before you wrap it. Give both of them laudanum for the pain."

Big Ed Creighton looked at Appling's body, his jaw trembling with the effort to control his emotions.

"Boys," he called out, "I got no money to pay fighting

wages. I won't hold it against any man who wants to draw his pay and light a shuck back east."

Taffy Blackford waved this offer aside. The Welshman was a big, blunt-jawed, rawboned man with curly red hair and whipcord trousers gone through at the knees. "Bottle that talk, boss. If you want to get up a posse to run those bastards down, deal me in."

Common troubles tended to knit men, and many others chorused agreement. It was a foolish, hotheaded idea, but Fargo had to admire these simple laborers. They were paid only a dollar a day, yet they were going full tilt to meet Western Union's tough deadline. Now and then jackass mail reached them, even less frequently warm beer, and on Sundays they rested and supped up on steak. But the other six days they worked from sunup to sundown. They slept on the ground, ate mostly bland and boring food yet kept their spirits high.

"You're all stout lads," Creighton replied, "but nix on the posse. Most of you have fired nothing but squirrel guns, and 'sides that, we've got no horses but dray nags. Fargo and Buckshot will settle accounts with these murderers, whoever the hell they are. We have an important job to do here, and as soon as we bury Danny we're getting back to it."

Creighton and his college-graduate secretary, Charles Brown, insisted on digging the grave themselves. After the brief, simple ceremony, gunpowder was burned over the grave to keep predators away. Work resumed and Fargo and Buckshot prepared their mounts for a possibly long, hard ride while discussing this new source of trouble.

"We riding out at sunrise?" Buckshot asked.

Fargo nodded. "That'll give them time to decide nobody followed them. And to get bored with waiting, happens they mean to ambush us."

"I hope we ain't up against one a them criminal armies like the Pukes and Jayhawkers raising hell back in Kansas and Missouri," Buckshot observed. "Big Ed is right about the workers being stout lads. But they'll dump the blanket in a big shooting fray."

Fargo, busy removing the Ovaro's horseshoes with a shoeing hammer, shook his head at this notion of an outlaw army. "Could be a bigger bunch somewhere, but don't seem likely to me. Those border ruffians back east live by raiding on settlements and robbing banks. If this bunch had enough men, they'd've raided us by now for our supplies."

Fargo rasped the stallion's hooves smooth, then trimmed them and nailed the shoes back on. Bad shoeing lamed more horses than any other cause. The smallest crack could work its way up from the hoof into the coronet, stranding man and animal. In country like this, that was a death warrant.

It didn't take Buckshot Brady long to warm to his favorite theme.

"Two bachelors of the saddle, Skye, that's us, lookin' to get our clocks wound by some willing strumpets. Way I kallate it, chumley, there ain't no more cathouses on this route. No settlement until we hit the end of trail at Camp Floyd, and that's Mormon country. Old Brigham's got him nineteen wives, but can horny bucks like me and you get even a sniff of cunny? Hell 'n' furies! I'm starting to look for knotholes in them telegraph poles."

"Why'n't you put a stopper on your gob?" Fargo snapped. "I don't need reminding we're in woman-scarce country."

"Skye Fargo going without poon," Buckshot roweled him mercilessly. "No wunner you been in such a scratchy mood. That's like a limey goin' without tea."

"You're a reg'lar caution to screech owls," Fargo retorted, his tone sarcastic.

Fargo checked the Ovaro for saddle galls, wiped the sweat from him with an old feed sack, then took a metal currycomb to him.

"That stallion is a huckleberry above a persimmon," Buckshot admired, studying the Ovaro. "Strong as a sheep man's socks. And smart? Well, I reckon! Yestiddy I seen him open the tailgate of the fodder wagon all by hisself."

Fargo pointed his chin toward the grulla. "Say, that little blue Indian cayuse of yours is some pumpkins, too. He'll stop on a two-bit piece and give you fifteen cents in change."

"He'll do to take along," Buckskin allowed. "I slit his nostrils for exter wind. Me, I prefer a mule in hard country. They'll gallop from hell to breakfast and back. Sure-footed, and they don't require tending like a horse. And if you're starving, mule meat is tastier. But a mule just ain't good company, and they ain't loyal like a good horse."

Buckshot spoke all this absently while he carefully inspected the smoky's feet. Now he said what was really on his mind. "Fargo, all three of them motherless cockchafers that opened up on us had repeating rifles. Sound like Spencer carbines to you?"

Fargo nodded. "I see you and me have hitched our thoughts to the same rail. You're thinking about all those snowbirds who deserted out of Fort Laramie and just disappeared?"

"The way you say. Signed up in the winter to get three hots and a cot without having to fight the red aborigines. Then, with the first spring thaw, they lit out to the west takin' their carbines and a shitload of ammo. Think this bunch today could be some of them yellow curs?"

"Distinct possibility," Fargo said. "That would explain the crime spree in this region. If that's the way of it, you might be right—there could be more than three of these sage rats. But I've scouted this entire area, and I just don't see any place where they could be holed up. No signs of old camps, either."

As if by tacit accord, both men gazed toward the freshly blackened earth that marked Danny Appling's grave.

"Man had him a wife and two pups on the rug," Buckshot mused aloud. "Sent his pay home reg'lar like. How will they get by now that he's been pegged out? The killing don't set right with me, Skye."

"We can't let it stand," Fargo agreed. "Come hell or high water, we can't let it stand."

At sundown Big Ed Creighton whistled the workday over. Several big campfires were built and decks of cards produced— poker, checkers, dominoes, and arm wrestling were the most popular pastimes during the few hours before the weary crews turned in for the night.

For a few of the men, however, work was just beginning. Cooks fired up their Dutch ovens to make hundreds of biscuits for breakfast, and wranglers tended to the dray horses. One man was even in charge of making soap, rendering lard with buffalo fat and lye. Once it hardened it was sliced into chips. It had to be rinsed off quickly or it would peel a man's skin.

Several whiskey barrels had been sawed in two to produce washtubs, for use when water was plentiful—which it hadn't been lately. Fargo eyed the wagon in which the washtubs were now uselessly stacked. Everybody was getting a mite whiffy, himself included.

The sound of drumming hooves approaching in the grainy twilight made Fargo and Buckshot snatch up their weapons. But a horn sounded loudly and all the men cheered. It was only a Pony Express rider thundering past.

"The brave lad on that horse will be out of a job when this line is finished," remarked Creighton in a regretful tone. He, Charles Brown, Fargo, and Buckshot were playing joker poker in the sawing yellow-orange flames of a campfire.

"Just as well," Fargo replied. "The Pony's losing money hand over fist. Five dollars to send a letter is bad enough. But I worked for one of the partners, Alexander Majors, and he told me the firm is losing twice that on every letter."

"Speaking of your former employers," spoke up Charles Brown as he frowned at his cards, "I read in *Police Gazette* a while back that Allan Pinkerton has joined the war as a spy for the Union side. Are you planning to enlist, Mr. Fargo?"

Brown was an earnest young man in his twenties who had been reading law in Omaha when Creighton hired him. He was also a devotee of half-dimers and "Wild West" magazines and, thus, in awe of the Trailsman. His formal, proper manner amused Fargo. But although there was plenty of green on his antlers, he was hard-working and eager to hone his frontier skills.

"Nope," Fargo replied. "I don't go in for slavery, but you have to take an oath to join the army. I won't swear an oath to any man or country. That just makes *me* into a slave."

Buckshot was trying to peek at Fargo's cards. Now he chuckled. "Fargo, you are the world-beatingest hombre I ever knew. You surely do measure corn by your own bushel. That's why I like you."

Fargo snorted. "Does this mean I'm spoken for?"

Big Ed and Brown hooted. Buckshot gave Fargo a mean squint. "I take it you're tired of eating solid food?"

"No looking at the deadwood," Fargo snapped when Buckshot reached for the discards pile.

The game progressed, bets limited to nickels and dimes. A talented banjo player named Shoo Fly Jones was picking out "Skip to My Lou" while some of the men sang along.

"Where you headed when this job's over?" Creighton asked Fargo. "I can get you a good job with Western Union—something more permanent than contract work."

"Nothing permanent for me, thanks," Fargo replied. "I like contract jobs just fine. I'm like Buckshot—we both got jackrabbits in our socks."

"They call you a rootless man, Mr. Fargo," young Brown piped up, "but that's sheep dip. You're anchored to the entire American West. There's no Vanderbilt mansion bigger or more magnificent than your home."

Fargo's lips twitched into a grin at the kid's enthusiasm. He talked like a book sometimes, but wasn't that the mark of a college man? "Well, Charlie, looking at it that way . . ."

"Sure," Creighton pitched in, his tone sly, "and Fargo's got more bedrooms in his home."

"Not lately," Fargo complained. "This job pays pretty good, but it does leave a man woman starved."

Fargo kept an eye on the Ovaro, ground-tethered nearby. Although perimeter guards had been posted, Fargo had more faith in his stallion—the best sentry he had ever known. If there were enough army deserters roaming these parts, a night attack in force was not out of the question.

Charles Brown tilted back his head to gaze into a dark velvet sky shimmering with countless stars. "Mr. Fargo, do you believe in an All-wise Providence?"

Fargo shrugged one shoulder. "I wasn't Bible-raised, Charlie. Truth to tell, I'm a pagan. But I do wonder now and then how everything got here. If this Providence you mention is so 'All-wise,' how's come there's so damn many fools in the world?"

Big Ed chuckled. "Bully for you, Fargo. My wife is pious and a fine woman. But I keep asking her—why is it that human beings invent gods by the dozens, yet we can't even create one worm? Still . . . like Charlie here, I look at that night sky and I have to wonder."

Buckshot lifted his left leg and cut a loud fart. "There's a kiss for alla you cracker barrel philosophers. All *I* wunner is if my next sporting gal will give me the French pox and force me to the mercury cure. *That* sumbitch burns, chappies."

This remark make Buckshot sigh in fond reminiscence. "Skye, that hoor I had back in Omaha, the one with the big wart on her nose? She was coyote ugly and smelled like a bear's cave. But by God, she was *willing*. Why, she—"

"Sew up your lips." Fargo cut him off. It had been many long, suffering weeks since Fargo had even seen a woman, and Buckshot's constant harping on the subject only made the deprivation worse.

Shoo Fly Jones laid his banjo aside and stood up. "Boys," he announced loudly, "I sniff water close by."

This remark occasioned a great stirring and to-do throughout the camp. Shoo Fly had earned a reputation as a "water witch," and it fascinated the men to watch him in action. While he retrieved his pronged willow branch, several of the men quickly made torches from small limbs tipped with rags soaked in coal oil.

Buckshot dug an anticipatory elbow into Fargo's ribs. He and Creighton were the only ones who had guessed about the secret arrangement between Fargo and Shoo Fly.

Shoo Fly began to wander in slow circles around the main camp, his homely, careworn face tight with concentration as he "witched," holding the willow branch out in front of him. The excited men kept hushing each other up so that Shoo Fly could concentrate.

Suddenly the end of the stick dove toward the ground.

"Dig here, boys," he called out. "You'll find good water."

Several of the men had brought shovels. In a matter of minutes one of them shouted, "Huzzah! He's done 'er again, boys! Break out the bathtubs!"

A cheer swept through the men.

"Skye," Creighton said quietly as he tamped tobacco into his pipe, "I want to thank you again. These men are awfully bored, and this is great entertainment for them."

"Thank my horse," Fargo replied.

Earlier that day the Ovaro's sensitive nose had located this underground spring. Fargo and Shoo Fly had cooked up this scheme back in the Nebraska Panhandle and worked it several times since then. Fargo enjoyed the ruse as much as the rest of the men.

While some of the men filled water casks, Fargo and Buckshot took a good squint around the outskirts of camp, checking with all the guards.

"We best knock up some grub for the trail," Fargo remarked as both men gazed south across the moon-bleached landscape. "I want to ride out before full light."

"You seen the notched trees in this area?" Buckshot asked.

"What, you think I'm as green as Charlie? How could I miss 'em?"

"I can't break their code," Buckshot said. "But it's Northern Cheyennes sending messages to their Sioux battle cousins. Messages about the paleface invaders crossing their ranges."

"They know every damn thing we're up to," Fargo agreed. "And they'll be watching me and you when we ride out."

"Paleface killers ahead of us and pissed-off savages on our back trail," Buckshot said. "*Thank* you, Jesus, for another glorious day siding Skye Fargo!"

3

The next morning, even before the dull yellow sun edged over the eastern horizon, Fargo and Buckshot tacked their mounts and headed due south, tracking their quarry across the vast stretch of southern Wyoming known as the Great Divide Basin.

The imposing Wind River Range of the Rockies saw-toothed the sky behind them, and smaller ranges encircled them. Much of the basin was a broad expanse of sage and greasewood bushes—and a bushwhacker's paradise. In places the sagebrush was tall enough to conceal a standing man.

Years of scouting dangerous country had taught both men a hair-trigger alertness that was as habitual as breathing. So far, tracking the trio of attackers proved easier than rolling off a log. They had taken no pains to obscure their trail, and the hoof depressions in the lush grass—overlapping often, the sign of a gallop—proved their greatest concern was fast escape, not concealment.

"As long as we can see all three sets of those tracks," Fargo remarked about an hour after they rode out from the work camp, "we don't have to worry about being dry-gulched."

"Ahuh," Buckshot agreed. "Seen any featherheads yet?"

"Nope. But you know how it is with Bronze John—we'll see him only when he wants us to. This is their range and they don't miss a damn thing. They're out there watching us."

The two men rode for several more miles in silence, each man alone with his thoughts. Then Buckshot abruptly spoke up.

"You know what, Skye? Eastern capital is the goddamn enemy of the westering man. Them sons-a-bitches back in

Washington City is powwowing with them railroad barons right now, cuttin' the West up like it was a pie baked just for them. This telegraph me and you is helping to string through—it ain't for the common man. It's just making things easier for the damn railroads when they finally come through."

"'Fraid so," Fargo agreed. "But Big Ed ain't in their hip pocket. He raised the money for this line himself after Western Union put it up for bid. And I think he *does* mean for it to help the common man."

"Nothing cheapjack about him," Buckshot acknowledged. "Him and Charlie both are straight grain clear through. Some of these big nabobs, why, hell! They want to rise so high that when they shit they don't miss nobody. Big Ed ain't like that."

Fargo agreed, but the westering fever was far bigger than one good man's intentions. It took at least five months for a wagon train to get from Missouri to Oregon, with one in ten pilgrims dying along the way. But at the moment, the "Wild West" was of no interest to most of them—it was just Zebulon Pike's Great American Desert that must be crossed to reach the supposed paradise of California or Oregon.

But that Western capital Buckshot had just cussed out was already at work, and Fargo knew it wouldn't be long until the Great Plains and Intermountain West peopled up, too—hell, the killers were obviously already here. The buffalo, the free-range Indians, and finally the drifters like him and Buckshot would be hemmed in on all sides.

"Might's well face it, old son," he remarked. "Men like me and you will likely end up our lives—if we don't die of lead colic first—holed up in Death Valley or the Jornada del Muerto. Surviving on rattlesnake and cactus juice."

Buckshot loosed a brown streamer into the grass. "Ain't it the drizzlin' shits? Soft-handed town bastards driving us out of our own country."

The trail of the attackers was still plain, still pointing due south straight as a plumb line. But Fargo briefly jogged west to avoid a level range pockmarked by prairie dog towns. A horse with a snapped ankle was the last thing they needed.

"Where in Sam Hill are these cockroaches headed?"

Buckshot wondered aloud. "Mayhap they got a camp on Bitter Creek. I been down that way tracking Injins—good water, good graze, and you can see anybody coming at you for miles."

"I hope not," Fargo replied. "Unless we sneak in at night, they'd shoot us to doll stuffings before we got across that tableland."

"Bad medicine," Buckshot agreed. He gnawed off a corner of his plug and parked it in his cheek as soon as he had it juicing proper.

"Chaw?" he asked Fargo, offering the tobacco.

Fargo waved it off. "Can't abide the taste."

"You damn weak sister. You gotta learn to chew the suption out of it, is all."

Buckshot loosed another brown streamer that just missed Fargo's boot.

"You get that *suption* on me," Fargo warned, "and you'll be wearing your ass for a hat."

Buckshot hooted. "Won'tcha listen to pretty teeth? The pup is barkin' like a full-growed dog."

The terrain gradually altered and soon the riders were crossing meadows where sunflowers grew shoulder high and blue-winged teals darted about like spring-drunk butterflies. The horses, never pushed beyond a trot, still had plenty of bottom. Fargo had lashed a goat gut filled with water to the Ovaro, and now the two riders reined in to water the mounts from their hats.

"Sheep clouds making up," Fargo remarked as they hit leather and gigged their horses forward again. "Rain's likely in an hour or two."

"I wunner when them Injins will show," Buckshot said, slewing around in his saddle to study their back trail.

"If it's Cheyennes," Fargo reminded him, "they'll likely show up on our flanks or out front of us. They don't track their enemies—they pace 'em and guess where they're headed."

Both men gnawed on buffalo jerky and cold biscuits in the saddle. When he finished eating, Fargo poked a skinny black Mexican cigar into his teeth and scratched a phosphor to life with his thumbnail. He leaned forward into the flame, fighting the wind for a light. The wind won and he cursed mildly, sticking the cigar back into his possibles bag—he was damned if he'd use up another precious match.

A few more uneventful miles and the terrain changed again, rising slightly as the grass thinned to sandy patches. Scattered rock spines dotted the land, and Fargo realized that was potentially dangerous news.

"Trouble," he announced, lake blue eyes slanted toward the ground. "They've pulled an Indian trick on us and split off in three directions."

Buckshot eyed the nearest rock spine, rubbing his chin. "And in good ambush country, too. One a them shit-heels could be layin' back to pop us over."

"Nothing else for it," Fargo decided. "I'd wager all three of them are headed to the same place, so it won't matter which trail we follow. Let's stick with the middle one."

"Hey diddle diddle and up the middle," Buckshot agreed. "That's how me, Kit, and Uncle Dick attacked and drove them Mexer freebooters out of Taos. Scattered 'em like nine-pins. Them pepper guts ran like a river when the snow melts."

"Way I heard it," Fargo said, "you were drunk as a fiddler's bitch and wallowing with a whore during that battle."

Buckshot sent him a dirty look and then expelled a sigh. "You're a hard man to bullshit, Skye. Well, I'll take a hoor over a shooting scrape every time."

Both men, realizing their increased danger with the trip split up, scoured their surroundings with an eye to likely snipers' nests. Fargo's earlier prediction came true when a sudden thunderstorm boiled up. Gray sheets of wind-driven rain pelted them, destroying visibility and forcing them to shelter under a traprock shelf. The rain lasted nearly an hour and left patches of mud as thick and sloppy as gumbo, slowing them down. But both men were among the best trackers in the West and they held the trail.

However, it was a rough piece of work. Splitting up was only the beginning of their enemy's precautions. The rider they were following also rode for several hundred yards through a small creek, making it difficult for his trackers to pick up the spot where he emerged. And once he even rode into a chewed up buffalo run, obscuring his tracks.

"I'm thinking maybe you were right yesterday, Buckshot," Fargo speculated out loud. "This jasper went to a lot of trouble to hide his trail. That tells me these three ain't just on the prod—they've got themselves a hideout and they're bound and determined to keep anybody from finding it."

The two men doggedly persisted, leaning low from the saddle and often forced to dismount to study the bend of the grass or an overturned stone. The afternoon heated up and biting flies plagued men and horses mercilessly.

"Shit-oh-dear," Fargo breathed softly when he and Buckshot rounded a long rock abutment. "Stay frosty, old son. Straight ahead and keep up the strut. Looks like we got company, and they don't appear too happy to see us."

Strung out in a line just ahead of them, impassive faces blank as gray slate, sat six Northern Cheyenne braves astride their mustangs, weapons pointed at the paleface intruders.

Fargo had expected an eventual encounter with one of the tribes, but had not envisioned riding cold into a trap like this. In his experience the Northern Cheyenne were not cold-blooded murderers, even of white men. Deeply religious in their fashion, the taking of a human life was not a casual act.

Then again, braves who had painted and danced, propitiating Maiyun the Great Supernatural, had a freer hand to take an enemy's life.

And every one of these braves wore his red, yellow, and black war paint.

"Katy Christ," Buckshot muttered, "I thought your stallion was trained to hate the Indian smell."

Buckshot meant the smell of the bear grease that Cheyenne braves smeared liberally into their long black hair.

"He is," Fargo replied quietly as they walked their mounts closer. "But we're upwind, you knothead."

"These red sons are painted, Fargo. How's 'bout I swing Patsy Plumb up and jerk both triggers? This smoke wagon can blow three of those bucks off their ponies. You're quicker than eyesight with that thumb-buster of yours—you can send the other three under faster than a finger snap."

"At least pre*tend* you got more brains than a rabbit. We leave six Cheyenne braves murdered and we'll touch off a vengeance war that'll guarandamntee Indian haircuts for Big Ed and his crew. *Don't* pull down on them unless we can't wangle out of this."

Fargo raised one hand high in sign talk for peace. Both men drew rein about ten feet in front of the line of grim-faced braves. The two men kept any feelings from showing in their faces—a white man's habit despised by most Plains warriors as unmanly.

The brave who first spoke had the most eagle-tail feathers dangling from his coup stick, making him the natural choice for leader.

"Mah-ish-ta-shee-da," he said in a tone laced with contempt—the Cheyenne word for white men. Fargo knew enough of their language to know it meant "yellow eyes"—the first white men the Cheyenne had ever seen were fur trappers suffering from severe jaundice.

Fargo thumped his own chest with his fist, a symbol of defiance—a reaction more likely to engender respect among these proud and defiant warriors.

"Wasichu," he said proudly, the Lakota Sioux word for white men and a language the Cheyenne knew well for the Sioux were their battle cousins.

Fargo noticed that all six braves avoided making direct eye contact with the white men, fearing they might steal their souls. He made a quick survey of the weapons now trained on him and Buckshot. One Cheyenne had a badly used .33 caliber breechloader, a standard trade rifle. Its cracked stock had been wrapped tightly with buckskin. Another held a cap-and-ball Colt's Dragoon pistol, a "knockdown gun" whose huge, conical slug often killed even with a hit to the arm or leg.

The other four brandished Osage-wood bows, arrows nocked, and light but deadly spears tipped with flaked-flint points.

"Why are you here, hair face?" the leader demanded in the Lakota tongue.

Fargo had long ago learned the universal sign language used by Plains Indians as a lingua franca between tribes. He replied using signs for Lakota or Cheyenne words he didn't know.

"The paleface believes the land belongs to him. Like the red man, I believe we all belong to the land. I belong to this place. It has always been my home."

The brave seemed momentarily impressed by this unexpected answer. But he had to save face with the others, so he shook his head adamantly. "From Great Waters to place where sun rises, white man's home. From Great Waters to place where sun sets, red man's home."

Fargo hooked a thumb toward Buckshot. "Look at him. He mounts his horse from the Indian side. You can see he is no hair face. He is Choctaw and his tribe is from east of Great Waters."

"You speak in a wolf bark! Where are these tribes now? Planting corn like women in the place where your white leader Sharp Knife sent them. No horses, no weapons. They are prisoners. And you plan to send us there and make women of our men."

The brave with the Colt's Dragoon thumbed his hammer from half to full cock. "I will kill the beef-eaters now!"

"Fargo," Buckshot said quietly but urgently, "our tits are in the wringer, boy. I'm swingin' Patsy up—you best jerk your short iron."

Before Fargo could reply, the leader raised his hand to stop the hothead. Then he addressed himself to Fargo.

"It is true that you look different than the Mah-ish-ta-shee-da who travel in the great bone shakers. You and your friend have not cut your stallions and broken their spirit. You wear buckskins. You know a little of our tongue. Your faces are not those of women who show their feelings. Perhaps you do belong to this place, and the Cheyenne Way does not permit us to kill you."

The immediate danger of violent action had passed for the moment, but Fargo knew they had avoided a stampede only to be caught in a flood. When Plains warriors spared a white man's life, they exacted tribute for crossing Indian ranges safely. Despite their obvious admiration for the Ovaro and Buckshot's rare grulla, the warriors knew it was beyond the pale to demand a man's horse in this country.

But the way they had been covetously admiring Fargo's Henry and Buckshot's double-ten, it was clear what was coming.

"You may go in peace," the brave continued, "but you will leave your thunder sticks with us. And that fine knife in your . . ."

He did not know the word for boot so he pointed at the Arkansas toothpick in Fargo's boot sheath. Fargo shook his head.

"Would you surrender your best weapons?" the Trailsman demanded. "We will give you some sugar and coffee. These are fine things."

This puny offer clearly angered the brave although his stoic face never altered. His eyes and voice hardened.

"Hair face, it is the white man's stink that scares away Uncle Pte, the buffalo. Your strong water makes women of our best braves. Even now the white dogs swarm the sacred Paha Sapa"—he meant the Black Hills to the east—"searching for the glittering yellow rocks. Why should we not kill you both and take everything you own?"

Fargo always favored wit and wile over lead slinging. But he feared the worst option was now the only option. Buckshot considered his beloved double-ten an extension of his body, and no man—red, white, or purple—was taking Fargo's Henry from him.

Fargo's thumb twitched, knocking the riding thong off the hammer of his Colt. "I hate to say it, Buckshot," he said in a low tone, "but it's come down to the nut-cuttin'. Get ready to let 'er rip."

But Buckshot had followed most of the exchange and now he spoke up. "Hold off, Fargo. 'Member what we done with them Arapahos up at Roaring Horse Canyon?"

Fargo did remember and suddenly grinned inwardly. It just might work, at that.

"You should take nothing from us," he told the angry brave, "because your medicine will go bad if you do. This man riding with me is We-Ota-Wichasa, a great medicine man. He has come to this country on a vision quest."

The leader's voice was mocking. "Words are cheap, things of smoke. Especially in a white man's mouth as he faces death. Let us see this great 'shaman's' medicine."

Fargo nodded and looked at Buckshot. The latter lifted his arms like a priest blessing his flock. In a solemn, deep-chested voice he intoned:

Had to take a shit so she squat on the floor;
Wind from her ass blew the cat out the door;
Moon shone bright on the tipples of her nits;
Carved her initials in a bucket of shit.

The Cheyenne understood not one word of this mysterious incantation, but, in spite of themselves, watched this supposed shaman with growing expectation. Buckshot whistled sharply and his cayuse performed a half turn, putting Buckshot's back to the Cheyenne. His right hand moved up to his face briefly.

He whistled again and the smoky turned back around. Fargo had never seen the color drain from a copper-skinned Indian's face, but he witnessed it now when the braves saw the raw red socket from which Buckshot's right eye had simply disappeared.

To cap the climax, his lips curled back to reveal his eye staring at the bucks from his grinning mouth!

The braves did not turn and flee—they were too astounded to even move. And every one of them forgot about the "stoic impassivity" of their faces as their jaws slacked open in astonishment when Buckshot made as if he were chewing.

"We-Ota-Wichasa has plucked out his own eye and now he eats it?" the leader said to Fargo in a wondering tone. "And there is no pain?"

Fargo shook his head. "A new eye will grow back by tomorrow."

"His medicine is indeed powerful."

The braves spoke rapidly among themselves. Then the leader raised his hand in the sign for peace before they raced off to the northeast at a gallop.

"Jesus, Buckshot, you are a holy show," Fargo managed before both men laughed so hard they almost fell off their mounts. Then Buckshot worked his glass eye back into the socket.

But as they gigged their horses forward again, Fargo added, "You know, Cheyennes are superstitious, right enough. But they're also smart. They might figure out they were bamboozled somehow and pay us another visit."

"That's all right," Buckshot replied from a deadpan. "I'll keep an eye out for 'em."

4

A hot westering sun had soon baked the mud into hard folds and wrinkles. But the recent downpour had made reading sign more difficult and slowed down the two trackers. Fargo still had to worry about the terrain, too. Rock spines, gulches, and thick brush provided excellent cover for any man with dry-gulching on his mind.

"They *still* ain't joined back up. These murdering scuts are going to a helluva lot of trouble to keep trackers off their spoor," Buckshot remarked as the two riders crossed through a line of sand hills. "What gets my money is them thinking they can stop Big Ed Creighton from stringing up that telegraph. Why, it's hog stupid. That stubborn Irishman could route Powder River uphill if he set his mind to it."

"It's not so stupid," Fargo gainsaid. "Remember, they *don't* know Big Ed. I was out in California when Mexican freebooters stopped a line going up between Sacramento and Los Angeles."

"I recall that," Buckshot conceded. "It was a big gang armed to the teeth. And mayhap there's a big nest of 'em out here, too. How do we play it when we find their hideout?"

Fargo backhanded sweat from his brow, eyes in constant motion. The latest hatch of flies was plaguing him and the Ovaro to distraction.

"Hell, where do all lost years go?" he replied irritably. "What's after what's next? Ask me something easy now and then."

"Ain't you the touchy son of a bitch now you ain't gettin' no poon? Look, you're the big bushway here. You telling me you ain't even got a mother-lovin' plan?"

"You know my anthem, hoss—the best way to cure a boil

is to lance it. I favor handling this deal ourselves. These are stone-cold killers, not a bunch of harum-scarum cowboys hooraying the town. This is a territory, not a state, and it looks like right now we're the only law around. If there's too damn many for us to hug with, well, I don't plan to get us killed in a lost cause. We'll have to reconnoiter, fix the location, and report it to Fort Laramie."

"Naught else for it," Buckshot agreed reluctantly. "Big Ed's got that pocket relay doodad. If the line is back up, he can send word. It chaps my ass though, Skye. The fort ain't likely to send out troops. Happens that's so, the scum buckets that killed Danny and shot up Steve and Ron will escape the wrath. Neither one of us got a gander at any of 'em. Didn't even glom their horses."

Fargo nodded, his lips set in a grim, straight line. Yesterday he had vowed the murder would not stand. He also believed it wasn't true bravery if a man took action only when he was sure of success.

"We're the only law, Buckshot," he repeated. "And we're both death to the devil in a scrape. Piss and vinegar has got us out of some tough fixes before. Straight ahead and keep up the strut, hey?"

"*Hell* yes!" Buckshot said, rallying. "No matter how you slice it, there's no laurels to be won. But I never planned to live forever—leastways, not after I met you."

The sun was a flat orange disk balanced on the western horizon when the two horsebackers reached a clear, sand-bottom creek meandering through a grassy draw.

"Good place to camp," Fargo decided. "But we best not risk a fire tonight—it's too open here. We'll build one tomorrow and get outside of some hot grub before we ride out. That is, if we can pull a fish out of that creek."

"Sun going low and no hot supper," Buckshot groused good-naturedly. "*Thank* you, Jesus! Another glorious day siding Skye goldang Fargo."

The two men loosed their cinches and pulled their saddles, then dropped the bits and bridles before tethering their mounts in good graze beside the creek. When the mounts had cooled off they'd be allowed to tank up. They spread their saddle blankets out in the grass to dry. Then they flopped on their bellies and dunked their heads in the cool, bracing water. Fargo spat out the first mouthful before drinking deeply.

"I druther have a bottle of rye and a jolt glass," Buckshot declared as he pushed back up on his feet and clapped his cavalry hat back on. "Been too damn long since we was on a carouse, Skye. 'Member that saloon brawl down in San Antone? You caught some riverboat gambler crimping his cards and thrashed him six ways to Sunday."

Fargo chuckled as he slid the Arkansas toothpick from its boot sheath and moved several yards down the bank, squatting on his heels.

"Yeah, and then you cold-cocked that sheriff's deputy when he tried to break it up. Got us a twenty-five-dollar fine and three days in the calaboose."

Fargo saw a flash of silver, cocked his arm back, and threw his toothpick in a fast overhand toss. When he retrieved it, a good-sized trout came up with it.

"There's breakfast," Buckshot said. "Damn, you're some pumpkins with that blade."

Before the last daylight faded the two men spread their canvas ground sheets, then their blankets, using their saddles for pillows. Knowing mosquitoes would soon plague them, they placed their oilskin slickers close to hand to pull over their heads.

They supped on jerky and Fargo's last airtight of peaches, sharing the sweet syrup.

"You and that damn hog-bristle brush," Buckshot carped when Fargo started in on his teeth. "I don't trust a man with pretty teeth."

"Maybe that's because the few you got left are the color of molasses," Fargo retorted.

"I expect them nice pie-biters draw the gals to you. That and all them fool ink-slingers puffing you up big in the crapsheets. Dead broke and famous—that's you, Fargo."

"Not famous," Fargo countered. "I've got a reputation. A famous man gets backslapped and stood to drinks. A man with a reputation gets shot at from dark corners."

"Why, that's so, ain't it? I never knowed a man to get

more lead chucked at him than you do. But there's no denying that pretty gals want you under their petticoats."

Buckshot cast a tragic sigh, and Fargo knew what was coming.

"You know, chum, a man can cut a new wick out of his long johns. He can repair a bridle with a fringe from his buckskins. He can even plug up a bullet hole with flour or gunpowder. But there just ain't no substitute for pussy. Yessir, the old crack of doom. Been too damn long since I done the function at the junction."

"Caulk up," Fargo snapped. "I'm horny as a brass band in New Orleans, and I don't need all your damn reminders."

"I can't help it. See, I need more cunny than most men does. I'm what you call concu—concu—concupisser or somethin' like that. Means I got to be fuckin' all the time, y'unnerstan'? It's been proved by them as knows."

Fargo rose up on one elbow, curious in spite of himself. "What the hell are you flapping your gums about now?"

"Down in El Paso I had my skull read by a bumpologist. They can tell all about a man just by feeling his skull and making up a chart of it."

"I don't have to touch your skull to know you're a knothead. Now pipe down and let me sleep."

For a few peaceful minutes Buckshot was silent. Fargo felt his saddle-sore muscles relaxing as the hum of cicadas rose and fell in a monotonous cadence. The birds had not yet settled in for the night and Fargo heard the harsh calls of willets and grebes and hawks, the softer warbling of orioles and thrushes and purple finches. The steady chuckle of the creek lulled him and his eyelids began to feel weighted down with coins.

Buckshot's tobacco-roughened voice jarred him back to awareness.

"Damn it, Skye, I been stewing on it. When the frontier goes this nation will turn flabby and old maidish. A great nation—why, it *needs* a frontier. A man has got to dream and wonder about what he'll find over the next ridge. When it's all mapped and fenced—why, pah! What will our tads in short pants dream of being—barbers' clerks and Philadelphia lawyers?"

This was a rare moment of somber reflection for Buckshot, and Fargo listened attentively. Buckshot went on. "Lookit how it is over in England and them old countries with kings and such—no room to swing a cat in, and a man can't even fart without every mother's son smelling it. I'm glad me and you was here for the shining times, but it puts a pang behind my pump to see how fast the old ways is being stampeded."

"It's not over yet, old son," Fargo replied. "Not by a jugful. True, men always eventually foul their nests. But the American West is a mighty *big* nest. I'll wager that even a hundred years from now plenty of it will still be mostly like it is today. Names like Caleb Green and Daniel Boone and Davy Crockett will still be writ large. The mountains and rivers will endure. Men will grow soft, but they won't forget what they once were—not too soon, anyhow. England still has Robin Hood and that ancient king what's-his-name, the one that killed the dragon. There's King Arthur and all his knights. Our American boys won't stop dreaming about the old heroes."

Buckshot was silent and Fargo figured maybe he was digesting all this. His next remark suggested otherwise.

"You know, Skye? Mayhap there'll be quim at this outlaw camp—some soiled doves whose tits ain't dropped yet. Why, we might—"

A menacing metallic click from Fargo's bedroll—the unmistakable sound of his Colt going to full cock.

"Let's grab some shut-eye," Buckshot suggested hastily, and Fargo was still grinning as he tumbled over the threshold into sleep.

"Hell, Little Britches," argued Butch McDade, "you're the one always banging our ears about how we oughta show more initiative."

"Yes, but *after* you clear it with me," replied Jenny "Little Britches" Lavoy. "I consider you two my lieutenants because you're the best men in this bunch. But lieutenants act at the whim of their commanding officer. I assume you still agree that's me?"

Jenny fell silent while McDade and Lupe Cruz, his favorite

partner in crime, raked hungry eyes over her across the crude deal table. She was shapely and petite, her thick coffee-colored hair pulled into a tight chignon at the nape of her slender white neck. Finely sculpted cheeks glowed like fall apples. Her navy blue dress with velvet cuffs made her look innocent as a school teacher—a deceptive image she deliberately cultivated.

"Why, hell yes, you're the boss," McDade finally answered from a throat suddenly constricted with lust. "We voted you mayor of Hangtown, didn't we?"

"Yes, and I'm no fool, Butch. A rising tide must lift *all* the boats, and that's why we all share in the profits of our various . . . enterprises. But this attack on the telegraph line was a dangerous mistake, and you should have discussed it with me."

Jenny, Butch, and Lupe Cruz had met in a crude tent saloon aptly known as the Bucket of Blood. The place had a grim, masculine smell: sweat, leather, harsh tobacco, cheap 40-rod. The patrons were mostly mean, dirty men who looked out at the world from lidded eyes and surly faces—and now those eyes were intently focused on Jenny, the eyes of starving men staring at a table laid for a banquet. But the two imposing figures standing just behind Jenny's chair—her "palace guard" as she called them—kept them from eating their fill.

"But you yourself complained about the damn telegraph going through," McDade objected. He was a muscular and sandy-haired man with arrogant, trouble-seeking eyes and a cruel twist of mouth that kept him from being handsome. "You said it could spell the end of Hangtown."

"I meant eventually, Butch—*eventually*. But your attack might have hastened our destruction."

"That's hogwash, Little Britches," McDade snapped. Then his eyes rose to the two figures behind her chair and he softened his tone. "I mean, hell, they're just a bunch of gutless wage slaves. 'Sides, me, Lupe, and Waldo done a first-rate job of confusing anybody trying to track us. And the way Hangtown is hid . . . hell, *Indians* ride past and don't even spot it in this gulch. You got nothing to fret."

Jenny smiled demurely, knowing how it worked on men.

"All that might be true—and then again it might not. According to bubbling hearsay, Butch, the scout for that work crew is Skye Fargo—otherwise known as the Trailsman."

This revelation had the force of a hard slap to Butch's face. He stared at Lupe. "Goddamn it, it all ciphers, 'mano. That jasper on the black-and-white stallion, remember? The buckskins, the Henry rifle, the close-cropped beard . . . I had a gut hunch about him, but I didn't place him with the name. It could be Fargo, all right, damn the luck."

Now Cruz spoke up for the first time since the meeting began, and Jenny inwardly shuddered. Although she was never foolish enough to reveal the fact, he was the one man in this snake pit whom she truly feared. Rumored to be the best knife fighter in Mexico, he had the soulless eyes of a reptile—shifty, horse-trader's eyes. The string of human ears around his neck resembled wrinkled pieces of old leather.

"This Fargo," he told McDade, "es un hombre muy peligroso. A very dangerous man, uh?"

"And a first-rate tracker," Butch said in a fretful tone. "The best. I'll order a few of the snowbirds topside for sentry duty. Sure as shootin' he'll find this place if he decides to follow us."

Jenny tossed back her head and laughed. "Well, I didn't mean to start the Panic of 'Sixty-one, boys! You read too many half-dimers, Butch. Do you believe in Paul Bunyan and the boogeyman, too?"

McDade flushed. "Lupe's right. Fargo is dangerous, and he ain't no tall tale. I was south of here in a mining camp called Buckskin Joe when Fargo depopulated half the camp."

These men in Hangtown were hard-bitten men who'd rather risk getting shot to doing honest work—just the kind Jenny needed now for the first phase in her ambitious plans. But controlling them was a delicate art, especially for a woman.

"What's this?" she teased. "My best men going wobbly on me? All right, so Skye Fargo is a dangerous man. Every man has his Achilles' heel."

Butch gave her a blank stare. "His what?"

"A weakness, Butch. A vulnerable spot that an adversary

can use to defeat him. And Fargo's Achilles' heel is women—especially beautiful women."

"I hear he's quite the hound," Butch agreed.

"And wouldn't you two agree that I qualify as a beautiful woman?"

Butch raked his eyes over her again, the tip of his tongue brushing his upper lip as if he could taste her. "Pretty as four aces."

"Not pretty," Lupe corrected him. "*Hermosa. Tan Hermosa que nunca.* The most beautiful woman I have ever seen."

She swallowed their praise effortlessly. "Thanks, gents. If Fargo is stupid enough to enter Hangtown, it's his funeral. I'm dangerous, too. By the way—who is that ugly cur at the bar who's been leering at me and touching himself every time my eyes drift that way?"

"Boots Winkler," McDade replied. "One of the snowbirds you put on the payroll."

"Is he pulling his freight?"

"Christ no. He's a damn shirker and he ain't got the mentality for the job. Drinks whiskey like he's a pipe through the floor, and his tongue swings way too loose. He was so drunk during that last raid that he passed out on the ride back."

"Isn't he the one who likes to beat up on the soiled doves? In fact, isn't he the main reason all four of ours escaped Hangtown?"

"He ain't the only one, but he was the worst of the bunch, yeah. He cut up that last Mexer gal you hired just on account she laughed at his little tallywhacker."

Jenny nodded as if filing that fact away. She had gone to great pains to provide sporting gals to bolster the men's morale—and as a safety valve so their pent-up lust wouldn't result in her rape. Winkler's barbaric behavior could not be ignored.

Now her voice became all business. "All right, give me your report."

"Well, that attack on the Fort Laramie paymaster went off without a hitch. We nabbed seven thousand in military script and didn't kill no soldiers."

"Good work," Jenny praised. "I can get fifty cents on the dollar for it."

"The Butterfield coach raid didn't go quite as smooth. They had an ace shooter riding messenger and he dropped two of our boys before we doused his glims. We done for the driver, too."

"Any gold on board?"

"Naw. But there was three sacks of mail, and we're pulling cash out of some of the letters. A couple hunnert so far. Even better, we nabbed a well-to-do couple from Boston dressed in fancy feathers. They oughter fetch at least a couple thousand in ransom. They're locked in the guardhouse with the others."

Jenny nodded approval. "Fortune favors the bold, not the nickel chasers. But I *don't* want those prisoners mistreated. If I hadn't rescued Jasmine, your men would have raped her to death. Remember, damaged goods sell low."

"Waldo Tate's in charge of them, and he makes sure they eat good and none of the men get near the women."

"Yes, Waldo—the third man in your little trio. I call him Nervous Nell. Where is the ratty little creature? Didn't he go with you on this telegraph line strike?"

Butch nodded, rolling his head over his shoulder to indicate the other side of Hangtown's only street, an expanse of muddy ruts. "When we got back he got a little too cozy with the Chinee pipe. We left him at the Temple to sleep it off. He is a mite on the nervous side, but he's a cunning son of a bitch and a top hand with a rifle."

While this conversation had gone forward, Butch was sizing up the largest of the two silent, formidable men who accompanied Jenny everywhere—even to the privy. He was simply called El Burro, a mestizo of mixed Mexican and South American Indian blood. He was a hulking brute of a man with a hard, flat, expressionless face and shoulders wide as a yoke. The mammoth ape towered several inches over McDade's solid six-foot frame and wore a machete in a sisal scabbard. Two Colt Navy pistols were jammed behind his bright red sash.

"I'm just a mite curious, Little Britches," Butch said. "Word has it that these two bodyguards of yours are . . . ahh . . ."

"They're both eunuchs," she supplied. "El Burro and Norton both."

"That word's too far north for me."

"It means," she explained bluntly, "that they have no balls. I believe the frontier word is 'alterated.' Their genitals, along with their tongues, were lopped off by Comanches just north of Laredo."

Butch and Lupe exchanged an incredulous glance.

"Jesus Christ," Butch said, downing an entire pony glass of whiskey.

"You might say they know how it's done," Jenny added. "They just can't *do* it. But that's not a problem with you, is it?" she added, batting her long, curving lashes at him.

"Oh, I got all my equipment," he assured her eagerly, "and more than my share of original sin. And speaking on that . . . ain't it been a while since you had you a man?"

"Too long," Jenny assured him. "But I'm very selective. The itch is on me, but they say the best stallion is the one who neighs the loudest in the rut. And I want only the best stallion in Hangtown."

"This stallion," Lupe put in, his reptilian eyes giving Jenny the fantods, "must he be a *white* stallion?"

"Only the best stallion," Jenny insisted. "Color or markings don't matter."

McDade's mean lips pressed together tightly. "Well, there ain't been too many women ever gave Butch McDade the go-by."

"*I* have broken so many bed boards," Lupe boasted, "that now I take my women on the ground like animals."

"You two are the only candidates," Jenny assured them. "But I warn you now—I have *very* unusual tastes in carnal matters. Tastes neither of you has ever encountered."

The second part of this statement was true. But Jenny had to struggle to keep a straight face at the notion of ever giving her favors to either one of these common, lice-ridden mudsills. However, she had learned long ago that men could be most easily led around by their hard peckers, and her ambitious plans required ironclad control over men.

Now that she had both of them so excited they were forced to shift on their chairs, it was time to cool their ardor—and teach them the fear of God and the folly of ever touching her without permission. And with the soiled doves now gone, the rest of these horny outlaws needed to learn the same lesson.

Again she glanced at the drunken, feckless Boots Winkler. He saw her staring at him and once again crudely rubbed his crotch.

"Boots!" she called in a musical lilt. "Come over here."

Every eye in the smoky, dingy hovel riveted on her. These men weren't "citizens," she reminded herself—they were easy-money lemmings, and the only thing they respected was brutal power. Boots staggered to the table, so corned he listed like a sinking ship.

"Somethin' I can do for you, Little Britches?" he asked suggestively.

"I get the distinct impression that you don't respect me."

Boots was so inebriated that his face was bloated like an image in a warped mirror. "Hell, that's putting it a mite strong. It's just, you're always carrying on like some railroad plutocrat. Seems to me you could divvy up the swag a little more generous like."

"You don't need money here, now do you? Nobody's charging you for that liquor, and your eats are free. You should thank me for holding your wages so you don't gamble them all away."

"Well, Christ, I ain't some snot-nosed kid. I can hang on to my legem pone."

"Butch tells me you're worthless. That you can't even stay sober on the job. And it was you who treated the whores so rough they had to run away."

Winkler grinned like a drunken ape. "Now see, that there's a libel on me. They was just scairt of my big pecker."

"Nobody gives you something for nothing, Boots, except your mother. And I'm not your mother."

"'Course not," Winkler japed, playing to the crowd. "I never wanted to fuck my mother."

He expected a huge laugh, but the grogshop was as silent as a graveyard at midnight.

"You've reached the River Jordan," Jenny said softly. "Hear the current calling your name?"

"You wanna spell that out plain?" he demanded belligerently.

"Certainly. I'll make it very plain."

She gave El Burro an almost imperceptible nod. What

happened next was so quick it was over before the rest even registered the fact. El Burro's massive piston of an arm drove the heel of his palm at an angle up into Winkler's nose, snapping the long bone with a noise like green wood splitting. The broken bone was driven straight back into his brain, buckling his knees instantly. He flopped to the crude plank floor, reduced first to a heap of twitching humanity and then seconds later a fresh corpse.

Blood spurted from his nostrils in two powerful streamers, slapping onto the floor with a sound like a horse pissing onto frozen ground. The noise was oddly obscene in the dead quiet of the saloon.

"Somebody please drag him out of here," Jenny said in a pleasant voice. "Even though he's already dead, string him up on the gallows with the others."

She turned back to Butch and Lupe, offering them a coquettish smile. Both men's faces were frozen masks. "Nerve up, boys. I would rather you hadn't attacked that work crew up north, but don't worry about Skye Fargo. Any crusading fool who enters Hangtown will soon be twisting in the wind with all the others who gave this place its name."

5

On the second morning after the attack on Big Ed's crew, just after sunrise, Buckshot built a fire with deadwood that gave off little smoke. From long habit he made the campfire Indian style by burning the logs from the ends, not the middle, to avoid wasting wood.

Fargo boiled a handful of coffee beans in his battered, blue enameled pot while Buckshot took charge of the trout Fargo had impaled the evening before. He gutted the fish on a flat rock, wrapped it in leaves, and tossed it into the hot ashes to bake.

"Christ, Fargo," Buckshot complained, "this damn coffee is too thick to swallow and too thin to chew."

"It's better than that river bottom poison you brew," Fargo retorted. "If it's so bad, how's come you've had two cups?"

"One cup gives me a bellyache. Two moves my bowels."

They finished eating and Fargo spilled the dregs of his coffee into the grass before rinsing his mess kit in the creek.

"Let's tack up and grab leather," he said. "With luck I'll get you killed today."

Fargo loosened the tether and let the Ovaro buck for a minute to shake out the night kinks before he tossed on the blanket, pad, and saddle and cinched the girth. Then he secured his bedroll under the cantle straps. The morning was cool and breezy, perfect riding weather. They picked up the lone rider's trail and resumed their southward trek.

"There's one thing stumps me," Buckshot remarked after they had ridden a few miles. "Why did these puke pails bother to attack the work crew? All they got to do is pick any stretch of the line to the east of here and pull it down."

"They'll likely do that, but it's only temporary. Western

Union hired repair crews for every sector. Our sewer rats were hoping to stop the project or at least delay it for a good spell by scaring off the workers. Don't forget, we ran 'em off before they could kill a bunch more of the men."

Buckshot nodded. "All that shines. Happens you're right, there's a good chance they'll attack the crew again."

"It's our job to prevent that," Fargo said. "I ain't making this ride for my health."

By midmorning they had topped a low rise and Fargo reined in. "Here's where the three riders joined back up," he announced, swinging down out of the saddle and tossing the reins forward to hold the Ovaro.

Buckshot joined him and the two men squatted on their heels, studying the ground carefully.

"Our man got here first," Fargo said. "It must be their regular rendezvous point—you can see he waited for the two flank riders. His horse moved around grazing, and the grass in some of those prints has sprung up higher. The other two got here a couple hours later, both about the same time."

Buckshot used the toe of his boot to break open some horse dung. "Almost dry—they were well ahead of us. Well, we knowed that, but look here, Skye—these horses is being grained. Grain ain't all that easy to come by out here."

Fargo nodded. "You mighta been right, old son. Looks to me like maybe they got a well-supplied hideout somewhere. If that's so, these three aren't likely the whole shooting match."

Fargo took his army field glasses from a saddle pocket and clambered to the top of a nearby rock cairn. He studied each section of the terrain long and hard.

"It's a poser," he finally said, lowering the glasses and climbing down. "The terrain south of here is mostly flat and open. I don't see any canyons, no thick patches of trees, no places for caves even. Maybe you were right and they're all the way down on Bitter Creek."

Now that the trail was again easy to follow, they thumped their mounts up to a long trot. Now and then Fargo again searched the land out ahead with his binoculars.

They rode through occasional meadows bright with blue columbine and white Queen Anne's lace.

"Pretty country," Buckshot remarked. "Makes a man wish he could paint it or write poems about it. That bumpologist down in El Paso? He said that I'm a sensitive son of a bitch."

Buckshot pinched his nostrils and blew out two thick streamers of snot. Most of it smeared his shirt, and Fargo shook his head in disgust.

They made good time as the sun rose straight overhead at midday, heating up. His grulla still in motion, Buckshot took the reins in his teeth, shifted his weight, threw a leg around the saddle horn and built himself a cigarette.

"I'm pure-dee bumfoozled about another thing, Skye," he said. "Happens these yellow curs *are* alla way down on Bitter Creek, why would they join up agin where they did? Hell, it's another full day's ride. Why not stay split up until they was closer?"

Fargo had already begun rolling that question around in his mind. "That's one nut I haven't cracked yet."

"Well, *both* mine is cracked. We been pounding our saddles straight for hours now. Let's spell and water the horses— I gotta drain my snake."

They drew rein in the shade of a leathery-leaved cottonwood. Fargo drank from his canteen before watering the Ovaro from his hat. Then he climbed up into the rough-barked cottonwood and took another squint through his army-issue field glasses.

"Pay dirt, Buckshot," he announced triumphantly. "I just spotted a man peeking out from some bushes. A little over a mile ahead of us."

"'Bout damn time. Just one?"

"Hang on . . . no, there's at least two showing."

"They look like owlhoots?"

"I'd say of the deserter variety," Fargo replied. "They're both wearing parts of army uniforms. Say! There's a third. It's priddy clear they're sentries, but what the hell are they guarding? There's no buildings, no camp, just a long line of brush."

"Mebbe a dugout?" Buckshot suggested.

"Could be, I reckon. Maybe hidden behind the brush. It

would have to be mighty damn big because I can't see any horses either."

"Can they spot our horses, you think?"

"No," Fargo said, still staring intently through the glasses. "There's knolls and little stands of pine between us and them."

"So what do we do? Sit and play a harp?"

"Right now we're neither up the well nor down. It's no use to ride closer after dark—we need to see what we're up against. I think we can get in a lot closer if we use the natural cover."

Fargo climbed down and both men quickly checked their weapons.

"We'll have to leapfrog one at a time in single file," Fargo said, swinging up onto the hurricane deck. "I'll go first and you ride in my tracks. You know how to cover and conceal, hoss. Do your best work—the cover is thin. We might have to dismount and lead our horses."

It was slow going, Fargo giving the Ovaro his head and letting him walk. With long years of hard survival savvy to guide him, the Trailsman used every possible terrain feature to his advantage. Hills, hummocks, trees, knolls, swales—with an unerring eye for reading his environment he advanced as close as he dared. For the last few hundred yards he dismounted to lower his profile, leading the Ovaro by the bridle reins.

A brush-covered ridge offered the last possible cover and he halted, waiting for Buckshot to catch up. Fargo was close enough now to easily make out the faces of the bored sentries. Now he counted at least four.

"We're paring the cheese might close to the rind," Buckshot greeted him, peering out past Fargo. "Say! You're right—where the hell's their horses?"

"Damned if I know."

"Them's snowbirds, all right," Buckshot said. "I can see at least two Spencers. So what's your big idea now?"

"The cat sits by the gopher hole and waits. We best tie off our horses. If we watch long enough we might get a better idea how many there are and why they're standing guard in the middle of nowhere."

They tied their reins to weak branches—otherwise, if the horses were spooked and bolted, breaking the reins, the two men would be in a world of hurt trying to control their mounts.

"This shit's for the birds," Buckshot carped. "We're so close that if one of our horses whickers them bastards will be right on us."

"Give over with the calamity howling. The way you take on, we might's well shoot ourselves in the head."

Buckshot patted the butt of his double-ten. "Sit by the gopher hole, my lily-white ass. I say we attack. You're the one likes to lance the boils. Take the bull by the horns, says Fargo. Straight ahead and keep up the strut, says Fargo. Between the two of us we got enough lead to sink a steamboat."

"First of all, we got no proof any of these jaspers attacked the work crew. Even if they did, we need to know where the hive is," Fargo insisted. "What if there is a dugout somewhere behind that line of brush? We got to know how deep the water is before we just dive in headfirst."

"Mebbe so," Buckshot conceded without enthusiasm. His favorite tactic was the hell-bent for leather charge.

For the next half hour the two hidden men watched carefully while buffalo gnats swarmed their faces. Then— "Riders coming in from the east," Fargo reported. "Maybe this is just an outpost."

He watched the rider, a Mexican astride a blood bay gelding, lope closer, expecting him to dismount and take a report from the sentries.

Instead, both men felt their jaws slack open when, without breaking stride, the rider simply disappeared as if the earth had swallowed him whole!

For several stunned heartbeats the two frontiersmen stared at each other, saying nothing.

"I baked that fish with what I *thought* was wild onion," Buckshot finally said. "You think maybe I used peyote by mistake?"

"It was no peyote vision, old son. I see how it is now. Either that's one hell of a big dugout or the beginning of a gulch hidden by all that tall brush. I've seen some in the

Black Hills and Snake River country like that—you prac'ly have to fall into them to know they're there."

"A gulch," Buckshot repeated, rubbing his chin. "Might be. You'd hafta be a bird to spot it."

"We need to somehow get a size-up of the place," Fargo decided. "If the gang's not too big, we'll burn 'em down. If there's too many—"

A sudden crashing and thrashing from the brush to their left made both men pivot toward the horses, crouching with rifles at the ready.

"Oh, hell," Fargo muttered, "here comes a fandango."

A black bear, full grown and weighing at least two hundred fifty pounds, had emerged into the open, aggressively woofing at this intrusion into its territory. Two things guaranteed to panic a horse instantly were fire and bears. Both horses reared up, neighing loudly, eyes rolling in fear until they showed all white.

They tugged their reins loose and bolted. Buckshot, a fast runner, tore after his cayuse, hoping to seize the reins. The Ovaro, who rarely deserted his master, ran off about fifty feet, waiting to see what the bear would do.

But Fargo realized the fat was in the fire. The shout had gone up from the sentries and already slugs were whiffing in atop the ridge as they advanced. Fargo cursed as he levered the Henry and returned fire from a standing offhand position.

A quick glance over his shoulder told him that Buckshot had failed to stop the cayuse. He was escaping to the east at a two-twenty clip. At least all the gunfire had sent the bear into hiding.

But as Fargo looked ahead again to resume firing, his heart sat out the next beat—mounted men were pouring out of the hidden gulch or whatever it was, more than he could count.

The enemy fire peppering his position was vicious and sustained. He felt a sharp tug as a slug passed through the folds of shirt under his left armpit. Bullets snapped past his ear with a sound like angry hornets, one of the slugs creasing his left cheek in a white-hot wire of pain. Fargo was forced to fall back, firing as he went, popping one of the snowbirds over.

But it was like trying to hold the ocean back with a broom, and the mounted attackers were pounding closer amid a thundering racket of fire. They expertly divided around both ends of the ridge to form a pincers.

Buckshot had joined him again, his face grim with the realization that they were about to be cut down. Trying to escape on the Ovaro would be useless—with two big riders, and the mounted attackers already riding a head of steam, they'd never get clear in time.

Fargo had learned long ago, in desperate situations just like this one, that a man had to keep his blood cool and his thinking clear. Like Buckshot, he had first learned wilderness survival at the side of the last generation of mountain men. And it was a mountain man tactic that flashed into his mind now.

"Skirmishers waltz!" he shouted to Buckshot, who caught on instantly.

The two men stood with their backs braced one against the other. In perfect synchronization they rotated clockwise in a continuous circle. Not only did this reduce two targets to one, it allowed them to keep up a deadly, methodical, sustained field of fire to all four flanks.

"Horses are as good as men!" Fargo roared out above the unbelievable din of battle. "They'll be chasing us soon!"

The Henry's huge magazine capacity and rapid-firing lever action were critical now. Fargo propped the stock in his hip socket and fired with deadly accuracy, first a horse, then its rider. The attackers were just out of effective range of Buckshot's double-ten, but his North & Savage repeater was nearly as fast as Fargo's Henry—the trigger guard was combined with the lever, and when Buckshot moved it the cylinder revolved and cocked the hammer.

The attackers, their blood up for a quick slaughter, were stunned when the two men were able to rack up several kills and break up the pincers. Both groups fell back in a confused moil, wounded and dying men and horses raising hideous shrieks.

"Now!" Fargo told Buckshot. "Break for my stallion!"

Bullets nipping at their heels and kicking up plumes of dirt all around them, the beleaguered defenders raced full bore to the Ovaro. Fargo seized the reins, vaulted into the saddle, and pulled Buckshot up behind him.

Fargo thumped the stallion with his heels and the Ovaro shot forward as if spring-loaded.

"Them cockchafers ain't giving it up!" Buckshot shouted behind him even as a bullet knocked the left stirrup from under Fargo's boot.

At first, even under a double load, the Ovaro's superior speed and endurance opened up a slight lead. Soon, however, the attackers began to slowly gain, bullets raining in more accurately. A yellow cloud of dust boiled up behind the pursuers.

"We can't outrun 'em!" Fargo called to his friend. "So let's outgun 'em!"

"Steal their women and fuck their horses!" Buckshot rallied behind him. "Put at 'em, Trailsman!"

Fargo had learned that when escape was impossible, a sudden surprise attack was often the best option. He wheeled the Ovaro and both men shucked out their short guns.

Raising war whoops, revolvers blazing, they charged into the teeth of the attack. A man twisted in his saddle, blood blossoming from his wounded arm. Fargo emptied his wheel, took the reins in his teeth, and popped in his spare cylinder. With his third shot the lead rider slumped in his saddle, his jaw blown half off, then slipped from his mount.

One foot caught in the stirrup so that his body bumped and leaped over the uneven ground, slamming his wound hard over and over and making him scream like a hog under the blade. This broke the momentum of the attack as his unnerved companions fanned out helter-skelter to avoid this two-man juggernaut of death.

Fargo reversed their dust and headed in the same direction Buckshot's cayuse had taken. Both men were so powder-blackened they wore raccoon masks.

"Skye," Buckshot said behind him, "me 'n' you has been invited to a few balls in our day. But *that* one caps the climax. You coulda knocked me into a cocked hat when all them sons-a-bitches come spittin' up outta the ground. My nuts still ain't dropped back into the sac."

"I figured we were celestial," Fargo admitted.

"We done some fancy shootin' back there. But if your stallion hadn't held like he done, them double-poxed hounds woulda turned both of us into sieves by now."

"No bout adoubt it," Fargo agreed.

"Mister, I mean this is the onliest horse of its kind!"

"He's a fine old campaigner," Fargo said, patting the Ovaro's sweat-matted neck. His bit was flecked with foam, but the stallion tossed his head as if it was all in a day's work.

"How you set for ammo?" Buckshot asked.

"My long gun's empty and I've only got five shells for it in my saddle pocket. I've got seven loads for my Colt in my shell belt. How 'bout you?"

"Six slugs for my rifle, six for my short gun, eight for Patsy."

"I never expected we'd be locking horns with a battalion," Fargo said in a tone of self-reproach. "We were numbskulls not to pack along more ammo. Say, there's your cayuse."

The grulla was calmly cutting grass out ahead of them.

"The spavined nag," Buckshot muttered. "What now, chumley? We ride back to the work camp? We ain't got enough Kentucky pills to waltz with that bunch agin. Next time they jump us, all we'll have is our dicks in our hands."

"Yeah, we'll have to steer clear of them. But damn it to hell anyway, Buckshot—we have to at least glom the inside of that hidden gulch or whatever it is. We can't even make a report to Fort Laramie if we don't."

Fargo placed one hand against the sky. "Four fingers between the sun and the horizon—about a half hour until sundown. The moon goes into full phase tonight and we should have a clear sky. I say we hobble our mounts well out and sneak in on foot for a reconnoiter after dark."

Buckshot shook his head in wonder. "Fargo, I do believe you'd slap the devil's face in hell. But I kallate we all gotta die once."

"Last time I looked it up in the almanac," Fargo agreed, "the death rate was still one per person."

6

The moon-washed Wyoming landscape was an eerie silver blue like a painting. Fargo and Buckshot Brady hobbled their horses in a well-hidden draw about a mile south of the outlaws' position.

"Ain't seen any vedette riders," Buckshot remarked as he blackened his face with gunpowder.

Fargo carefully wiped out the bore of his Colt with a clean patch. "I'd wager they figure they ran us off for good."

Buckshot grunted. "A-course. That's what two *sane* men would do after that little cider party today."

"Always mislead, mystify, and surprise your enemy," Fargo retorted. "They'll likely have sentries out like they did earlier, but they won't really expect trouble. Like you say— sane men would skedaddle after realizing the odds. By now they're likely drunk as the lords of creation."

"I wunner if any of them three that attacked the work camp and killed Danny was amongst them we killed today," Buckshot said. "I sure-God hope so."

"Kill one fly, fill a million," Fargo replied.

Buckshot cursed and slapped his neck. "Case you ain't noticed, it's the skeeters' turn now."

Fargo glanced at the fat ball of moon. A man could tell the approximate time by it; a full moon was pure white early at night, and turned more golden as the night advanced, lightening to white again just before dawn.

"It's around midnight. Let's head out."

Knowing they might have to low-crawl, both men left their rifles with the horses although Buckshot, as always, refused to part with his beloved Patsy. Sticking to shelter when possible they covered the first half mile at a fast route step.

Soon they were close enough to see the orange-glowing tips of cigarettes marking sentry positions. As Fargo had predicted, the men were drunk and making no effort to hide their presence. Fargo could hear them roweling each other and laughing.

He and Buckshot moved in at a crawl for the last eighth mile, the flinty soil tearing at their knees, huge mosquitoes as big as a man's thumb-tip playing hell on their exposed skin. At times maddening swarms of gnats forced them to close their burning eyes until tears streamed out.

Fargo aimed for a spot between two sentry posts, coming in low now like a wriggling snake. The protective growth was a thick wall of wild plum and chokecherry bushes. The two men penetrated it and got their first good view, in the generous moonlight, of what lay below.

"Well I'll be hog-tied and earmarked," whispered Buckshot.

As Fargo had already surmised, a gulch—a narrow, shallow, three-sided canyon tapering to a spear point at its west end—lay below them. A crude facsimile of a town filled it. Several of the "buildings" were just stones piled up against the sides of the gulch to save on building back walls; others were clapboard shanties with oiled paper for windows and stiff cowhide doors hanging lopsided on leather hinges. There were a few large army tents and, at the far end of the gulch, a solid limestone structure that seemed luxuriant compared to the rest.

"That limestone building has no windows but plenty of loopholes," Fargo observed. "I'd guess it was built by fur traders for a winter quarters back in the day. Why the hell else would anybody even be here?"

"Ahuh. The Rocky Mountain Fur Company had trappers all over this neck of the woods."

"No awnings or duckboards anywhere," Fargo noted. "No church, no school, no hotel. This is no town, Buckshot. It's a vermin nest—the biggest one I've ever laid eyes on."

And damn near invisible from up on ground level, Fargo realized. This thick growth along the entire rim of the gulch guaranteed this. The rock-strewn terrain around it, dangerous for horses, would discourage riders from even getting near it. Fargo knew of several robbers' roosts in the West, but none that was actually a hidden town.

Buckshot's hand suddenly gripped Fargo's shoulder like an eagle's talon. "God's trousers, Fargo! Look just past the entrance to the gulch."

Fargo did and felt his scalp tingle. A crude gallows had been erected, and the bright moonlight showed a ghastly sight: three men in varying stages of decomposition, swaying gently when the breeze gusted.

"I reckon that's the welcoming committee," he said in a grim tone.

A leather case over Fargo's left hip held his 7X binoculars. There was adequate light, so he pulled them out and focused them on the corpses.

"The one on the left is priddy near a skeleton," he reported to Buckshot, "but the one on the right looks fresh-killed."

Fargo saw a couple dozen or so horses gathered in a pole corral near the gallows. The single street—actually just a mud wallow—showed little activity. But one of the big tents appeared to be a gathering place. Oily yellow light spilled out of the open entrance, and he could hear drunken voices shouting and cursing. There were even the raucous notes of a worn-out hurdy-gurdy.

The dark, square structure of rocks beside the big tent caught Fargo's eye. A guard was perched on a barrel in front of it, a rifle balanced across his thighs.

Fargo was still watching the building when he heard it— the unmistakable sound of a small child's cry of misery.

"Shut that puling whelp up!" the guard snarled through the doorway of the crude structure. "Or else I'll brain the little shit against a rock!"

Fargo cursed. "Well, that tears it, Buckshot. Big Ed told me the Butterfield kidnappings include a husband and wife with a one-year-old girl. That's gotta be the place where they're all held prisoner. Ed ain't gonna like it, but we can't just report this roach hole to soldier blue and walk away like it's none of our business. We got to handle this deal ourselves."

"Big Ed ain't gonna like it, huh? Great jumpin' Judas, Fargo, I don't like it neither! Sometimes I think you're at least a half bubble off bead. We ain't even drawing fightin' wages. I signed on to help you hunt and scout, not to do the mother-lovin' army's job. Boy, there's only *two* of us! Didn't that cartridge session today learn you nothin'?"

"No, because I learned it long ago—any son of a bitch who tries to kill Skye Fargo will end up shoveling coal in hell. I never marked you down for a chicken-gut, old son."

"Fargo, me 'n' you is chums, but you best ease off that sorter talk."

"Like hell I will. If those prisoners were all grown men, well, that'd be different. Men know this is harsh country, and they have to face up to their choice to be here. But women and kids—especially kids—got no choice in the matter. We're strong men, Buckshot, and by the code of strong men out West, we're duty bound to help those who can't fight for themselves. You know that, hoss—you're cussed ornery but a decent man. These whoreson shirkers will collect the ransom and then kill the whole family. Right now, like it or not, that kid is *our* kid."

Buckshot was quiet while a sudden wind gust shrieked through the gulch.

"Hell, Fargo," he finally said, his tone gruff, "no need to have a hissy fit. I'm with you right down to the hubs. But we need to stock up on ammo and parley with Big Ed."

"Yeah, we're heading back tonight. First, though, I want a closer size-up of that limestone building at the far end. I'd wager whoever lives there is the head hound in this pack of curs."

Fargo and Buckshot moved back out into the open country, hooked around to the west end of the gulch, and again slipped past sentries and penetrated the thick concealment of brush until they could peer over the rim.

The view thus revealed was a far cry from the filth and crudity of the rest of the gulch. The area behind the solid limestone building stretched between both narrowing walls of the gulch, forming a huge triangle completely out of sight except from overhead. Roses climbed a trellis against the house. Despite the late hour, several lanterns burned on wooden stands circling one of the new metal bathtubs that were shaped like coffins instead of barrels.

Fargo did a double take when a towering, stone-faced mestizo with a machete over his hip came out of the house and poured steaming water from a bucket into the tub. He was followed by another man, of medium height and solid build, likewise armed with a machete, who poured a second bucket of steaming water into the tub. Both men, Fargo noted, wore two Colt Navy sidearms jammed into sashes.

"Are them dumb gazabos takin' a bath this late?" Buckshot whispered. "Why, the night air has got a snap to it. The one with the flat map is big enough to fight cougars with a shoe. He won't fit in that tub."

"I'd say those two are servants or bodyguards or some such," Fargo whispered back. "Looks to me like the topkick of this shit pit is about to enjoy a soak. Maybe the two of us should drop in on him and make him the meat in a six-gun sandwich."

"Now you're whistling."

The two men brought out one more bucket of water each and returned to the house. A moment later the solid slab door opened again and Fargo forgot to take his next breath. The petite woman was so stunningly beautiful she mesmerized even the vastly experienced erotic acrobat whose amorous escapades were often hinted at in the penny press.

She wore only a thin linen wrapper and carried a porcelain jar. The beauty poured powder from the jar into the bath water, and Fargo realized this lass didn't let lye soap touch her creamy skin—even from fifteen feet above her Fargo whiffed the lilac scent of her exotic soap.

"Gol-*dang*!" Buckshot whispered hoarsely in his ear. "Skye, she's gonna get nekkid right in front of us!"

"Hush down, you fool," Fargo warned him. "Just enjoy the show."

She reached behind her neck and removed the tortoise-shell comb holding her dark brown hair in a chignon. It cascaded down around her shoulders as she untied the sash of her wrapper and let it fall in a puddle around her dainty feet.

Buckshot couldn't restrain himself. "Wouldja *look* at the

jahoobies on that little filly, Skye! Oh, Moses on the mountain! Right off them French playing cards!"

"Damn it, pipe down," Fargo whispered back. "She's got ears as well as tits."

But in fact he was looking, all right, forced to roll onto one hip as hot blood surged into his man gland.

Her tits were full, hard, and pointy, the strawberry nipples hard from the cool air. Her loose hair curtained one of them, just the pointed nipple peeping out provocatively between the dark tresses. Fargo's eyes slid over the flat, alabaster stomach to a triangle of dark mons hair. When she raised one leg over the edge of the tub to get in, he caught a quick glimpse of the soft inner petals of her sex.

His breathing was ragged and uneven now as the pent-up rut need brought out the savage stallion in him. But even with lust depriving his brain of blood, he noted something odd—the stunning brunette beauty had not removed the string of pearls she wore around her neck. As soon as she had adjusted to the hot water and relaxed, he found out why.

She pulled the pearls over her head and, slowly at first, began rubbing them one by one across both of her nipples. She began rubbing faster, ever faster, until her breathing matched Fargo's. When she had aroused herself sufficiently, she raised both legs, hooking one over each edge of the tub.

Buckshot was whimpering by now, and Fargo jabbed him with an elbow.

She slid the pearls down into the water and began the same treatment between her legs, many hard pearls rubbing one soft one. Her head rolled back and forth on the edge of the tub, she began to pant, then to groan. Suddenly she cried out as a climax shuddered her body.

Fargo was so stunned and aroused that he almost failed to restrain Buckshot in time when he started to lunge up.

"Damn it, Skye, let's *both* bull her right now!" he whispered, the sound almost a plea.

"Settle down or I'll shoot you," Fargo warned.

"Settle down, my sweet aunt! My dick is hard 'nuff to quarry with. Oh, to be them pearls!"

Before Fargo could reply, the languid beauty in the tub called out, "Jasmine! Warm up the water!"

A minute later a willowy blonde in a white gingham dress emerged from the house and poured more steaming water into the tub.

"C'mon, sugar britches," Buckshot urged under his breath, "shuck off that dress and climb in the tub with Pretty Pearls. Grind them tits together, gals."

But his Isle of Lesbos fantasy was dashed when Jasmine merely returned to the house.

"We've seen enough. Let's vamoose," Fargo said.

"She ain't done," Buckshot complained.

"I've seen all I can take, old son. She's a beauty, all right, but horny as I am, just *watching* her is like staring at a fresh-baked pie when I'm starving and knowing I can't have a slice."

"Yeah, I take your drift," Buckshot said. "I got me one helluva bellyache."

The two men carefully threaded their way through the protective ring of plum and chokecherry brush. They crept out into open country, eluding the sentries, then headed back to the southeast toward their horses.

"Tell me," Fargo said in a sly tone, "are you still reluctant to come back here?"

"We got us a duty to them prisoners," Buckshot asserted, suddenly eager and sanctimonious. "Why, the pond scum in that gulch is holding little children! You know us Western men got us a code."

Fargo chuckled. "Uh-huh. *Now* you come to Jesus."

"Skye, that gal in the tub—you figure she's one a them whatchacallits, a coocoobine? You know, a fancy whore for the man who runs the whole shebang in the gulch?"

"Concubine," Fargo corrected him. "Well, it don't seem likely a woman could be ramrod of a cutthroat bunch like that. Especially a woman who looks like her. I've seen out-laws' whores, and they sure's hell don't look like that little muffin. Nor that pretty blonde, neither."

"Ahuh. But you heard of Brasada Betty, ain'tcha? And Belle Winters. Both them gals was pistol-packin' mamas that run criminal outfits."

"True, but they both looked like fifty miles of bad road. I do remember a run-in with a pretty gal from New Orleans who was heisting banks in the Kansas Territory. But this . . . well, hell, there's a woman in charge of England. That gal in the tub just might be the big chief."

Whatever she was, Fargo resolved, after what he'd seen tonight, her naked body was painted on the back of his eyelids. And once a woman got stuck in his mind, he made it a priority to merge with her flesh.

"I never knowed that women diddled theirselves like that," Buckshot added. "Why, she was pettin' her own pussy."

Fargo snorted. "I s'pose you think they all sleep with their hands outside the blankets, huh?"

"Why wouldn't they? And how's come it looked like she got her rocks off like a man does? Now, ain't that uncommon queer? I mean, all they got down there is a hole, am I right?"

"You mean to tell me you don't know . . . ?"

Fargo trailed off figuring this was no time for a lecture on the female "magic button." Since Buckshot was a confirmed whoremonger, enlightenment would be wasted on him.

Just before they reached their horses Buckshot spoke up again. "Skye, you've bedded plenty of women. Have you *ever* seen anything like what that gal done with them pearls?"

"No," Fargo replied, a note of wonder creeping into his voice, "I never have. Makes you wonder what else is in her bag of tricks."

7

With no need to constantly read sign, and a bright full moon, Fargo and Buckshot held their mounts to a lope and made good time heading north. Fargo allowed for two days additional progress on the telegraph line, veering slightly west. By late morning they reached Big Ed Creighton's work crew.

"Damn, am I glad to see you two," Creighton greeted them before they even dismounted. He hooked a thumb over his shoulder. "We've got visitors."

Fargo aimed his gaze past Big Ed and a grin eased his lips apart.

"Look yonder, We-Ota-Wichasa," he told Buckshot.

The same six Cheyenne who had demanded tribute from the two men just two days ago now sat in a circle wolfing down hot johnnycake and slurping coffee. Their obvious zeal for the eats contrasted humorously with their carved-in-stone, expressionless faces.

"Give you any trouble?" Fargo asked as he lit down and dropped the Ovaro's bit and bridle before loosening the girth.

Creighton shrugged. "There's too many of us for them to threaten, I guess. They don't know a lick of English, so I can't cipher out why they're here—except they keep pointing out the telegraph poles and shaking their heads. You don't need to go to the blanket to know what that means. They do claim this land, after all. Say, who's We-Ota-Wichasa?"

"Just play along," Fargo said. "The way they're shoveling it down, I'd guess that grub has got them in a good mood."

"I'm glad I ordered a few cases of Gail Borden's new condensed milk," Ed said. "They're death on it—they keep dumping that and sugar in their coffee. They're tying into the pancakes full chisel, too."

When the braves saw Fargo and the powerful shaman We-Ota-Wichasa walking toward them, they rose uncertainly from the ground. All of them avoided eye contact, especially with Buckshot, although they sneaked quick peeks to see if his eye had grown back.

Fargo raised his right hand in the peace sign, addressing the leader with the most eagle-tail feathers on his coup stick. Again he mixed sign talk with Lakota and Cheyenne words.

"These wasichus have received you with respect. Their big chief wants to know what you wish from them?"

The brave, still chewing his food, seemed embarrassed after the hostile and ferocious show two days earlier. With obvious regret he set his delicious coffee down to talk.

"We are not here to make he-bear talk," he told Fargo. "We smoked to the four directions with the big chief. But this land is Lakota, Cheyenne, Arapaho land. Why are these yellow eyes cutting down our trees? Why do they strip the bark and branches and then plant them again in this odd row? And this hard sinew they tie between them for the birds to sit on—why are they doing these odd things?"

Fargo could tell the brave was far more curious than angry, and this was a good sign. It suggested they believed the white man's medicine was behind these baffling actions, and Fargo had to play to that belief.

"The white men," he explained, "know how to turn their words into lightning. The lightning courses through the hard sinew. Just as your tribe sends messages a great distance with smoke, the white men use this lightning."

The braves discussed this among themselves. Their leader turned to Fargo again.

"We have seen that We-Ota-Wichasa's medicine is strong. But Indian blood runs in him and places him close to the spirit in all things. We do not believe white men can send lightning through this sinew. Lightning comes from the god who first made days and gave them to men. He is the red man's god—he would not give his lightning to the white tribe."

"Ed," Fargo said, "do you have a good battery in one of the freight wagons?"

"Sure."

"Would a shock from it hurt a man?"

"Nah. Just jolt him a mite. Sort of a tickling tingle."

"Mosey on over there and get ready to connect the wire," Fargo said. "Don't let these wampum merchants see what you're up to. When you see me put my left hand on my hip, let 'er rip."

Fargo led the Cheyenne over to the unstrung portion of wire still lying in the grass. He handed it to the leader of the braves and instructed the rest to place a hand on their leader's arms.

"You will feel the lightning," Fargo told them. "It will not hurt you. But just as there is living spirit in the motion of the wind, there is life in this hard sinew."

"This is not possible, hair face," the brave insisted. "My people will band with the Lakota and other tribes. Together—"

Fargo placed his hand on his hip as the brave kept talking.

"—we will topple all these . . . *aiii*!"

As one the six braves leaped like butt-shot dogs. The leader threw the wire down. "Like a snake it bit me!" he exclaimed. "I could feel the life in it. You spoke straight arrow. This spirit life leaped through all of us."

Fargo nodded. "This is not the magic of those who live by night," he said, meaning black magic. "It will not harm the red man so long as he respects it."

Fargo said no more. This was a life force the Cheyenne could not fully understand, strong medicine indeed. Soon the word would spread across the West to many other tribes. Fargo predicted they would not touch these poles or wires even if they declared all-out war on the pale, hair-face invaders.

Before the Cheyenne rode out, Big Ed made them a gift of coffee beans, sugar, and the canned milk they had instantly taken a great fancy to.

"Good work, Fargo," he praised. "They ain't exactly swapping spit with us, but they're not on the warpath, either. Say, you fellows look beat out."

Creighton glanced over at the cook who had just fed the Indians. "Hiram, keep that Dutch oven hot and fry up a couple of the Sunday steaks."

Fresh meat was scarce with both of the hunters gone for

the past two days. But the choice steaks for the Sunday meal were kept cool on ice packed between layers of sawdust in a specially insulated wagon.

While they waited for their food, Fargo and Buckshot drank coffee and filled Big Ed in on their encounter down south on the Great Divide Basin. The only details Fargo omitted were the beautiful minx in the bathtub and her pretty blond companion named Jasmine.

Big Ed listened carefully, picking his teeth with a sharpened twig.

"A hidden town full of criminals," he said when Fargo fell silent. "Man alive! Sounds like you boys had quite a frolic down there. It's too bad you can't be sure you eliminated the three men who killed Danny, but it's still good work. I'll telegraph Fort Laramie."

"It won't do any good," Fargo said. "Soldier blue has lost too many men called back to this War Between the States. There's civilians at the fort they have to protect from Indian attacks."

"It's all we can do, Trailsman. That situation down south is none of our mix. It's a chance you have to take once you leave the States."

"Ed," Fargo said patiently, "those hard tails cut down Danny in cold blood. Are you saying murder is small potatoes?"

"Of course not, Skye. I'm the one had to write to his widow. But you of all people know that life on the frontier is a roll of the dice. It sounds cruel to say it, but human life is cheaper out here than it is back in the land of steady habits."

Fargo nodded. "That's true for Danny. He was a grown man. But, Ed, there's women and kids being held prisoner."

Creighton scowled. "Hold on here. All that is beside the mark. Are you by any chance telling me you're going back down there even if I say no?"

"'Fraid so."

Creighton looked a question at Buckshot.

"Sorry, Big Ed. Mebbe I need my head examined, but I gotta string along with Fargo," he said.

Creighton slowly shook his head as if shaking off a blow. "But I *need* my hunters and scouts. The men feel a lot safer with you two around. Fargo, those writers always say your word is your bond."

"Yeah, and part of the contract I signed says I'm to protect this crew and the telegraph line. Well, seems to me the biggest threat to it right now is that criminal bunch hiding in the gulch. And I don't lie down on any job I'm hired for."

Big Ed began to pace, his face agitated. "I've got eleven hundred miles of line to string by this fall. The newspapers ballyhoo the fact that me and Jim Gamble get a forty thousand dollar subsidy for ten years if we complete this line. But they never mention that we don't get one dollar of that money until the line is finished and operating."

"I know all that," Fargo said. "I also know you plan to use that money to build a college out West, not to put on airs."

"Do you also know that we're already having trouble meeting payroll? Jim has the hardest stretch, but he'll finish his four hundred and fifty miles because it's mostly hot desert. But if my crew gets bogged down in winter out here, there goes the whole project right down a rat hole. I *need* you two up here."

"Hell, it ain't like we're quitting," Fargo said. "Far as meat, you've got men who can drop small game—there's rabbits, wild turkeys, and such aplenty in this country. Far as scouting, you and Charlie know the route. The only other possible danger is Indians, and there's no sign they're greasing for war."

"What," Big Ed demanded, "could the two of you hope to accomplish against a town full of criminals?"

"I'm still cogitating on that," Fargo admitted.

"Fargo, you and Buckshot are not the law. I'm the boss here, and I'm holding you to the terms of your contracts."

"Way I see it, I'm meeting those terms," Fargo insisted. "This bunch won't stop sabotaging the line. Sure, you'll soon have repair crews. But they can't be everywhere at once, and what good's a telegraph that don't work half the time?"

Creighton's jaw muscles knotted. "Like I said, I'm the boss. If you two ride out against my orders, don't bother coming back."

He stalked off.

"Ain't *he* in a pet?" Buckshot said. "I never figured Big Ed for the kind who'd turn his back on the murder of his own men."

"He's got more starch in his collar than you credit him with. Maybe he'll cool off and see it our way. Well, let's stoke our bellies and grab some shut-eye. Our horses need a full day's rest, so we'll set out at sunrise after we stock up on ammo."

Buckshot nodded absently, his mind on something else. "I just don't unnerstan', Skye, what the *hell* she was doing with them pearls."

Fargo gave a weary grin. "I do, old warhorse. I do."

While the two men slept, the telegraph line advanced several miles. The sound of a horse approaching woke Fargo up, his Colt to hand even before he'd blinked away the cobwebs of sleep.

"The hell's this?" Big Ed greeted him with a broad smile. "First you rebel on me, now you're gonna shoot me?"

Fargo grinned as he leathered his shooter and rose to his feet, kicking Buckshot awake. "Stir your stumps, mooncalf! What's on the spit, Ed?"

"Tack up and come join the rest of us for supper," Creighton said. "It's almost sundown."

As the two men prepared to ride, Creighton took in a deep breath. "Fargo, have you ever heard of this fellow Thoreau?"

"Seen the name here and there," Fargo replied. "Went to the hoosegow for not paying his taxes, didn't he?"

"Ah, that was just for show—he knew his friends would pay it for him. But he's a fine writer and rates aces high with me. He wrote this one line that reminds me of you: 'A man more right than his neighbors constitutes a majority of one.' You're right about riding south, Skye. You wouldn't be the Trailsman if you didn't."

"Yeah," Buckshot muttered in a whisper, "but you didn't tell him about the little hussy in that bathtub."

As the trio followed the newly strung line west, Ed said, "Fargo, I still think it's plumb loco for just the two of you to take on so many. My workers have enough sand to stick it out even if a few volunteers go with you. A few of these men have been soldiers or fought Indians."

"Thanks, Ed, but me and Buckshot found out yesterday what will happen to men without excellent horseflesh. Besides, this deal will have to be done by wit and wile, not frontal assault. It'll be easier for two men to move around and conceal."

"Well, I say let a man go the gait he chooses—especially when he's the expert in these matters."

"You just keep pushing west," Fargo said. "If me and Buckshot play this right, we won't be long in returning. I know money is a big problem for you, so just keep setting those poles."

"Ahh, like my wife is fond of telling me—it's a long lane that has no turning. Money be hanged! I've got Horace Greeley and his *New York Tribune* in my camp."

"If he *was* in your camp," Fargo quipped, "he'd be picking weevils out of his hardtack instead of eating oysters and ice cream at Delmonico's."

After supper the men broke off into their usual groups to play poker, checkers, and dominoes.

"I wunner where Shoo Fly is," Buckshot remarked. "Usually he's playing his banjo 'long about now."

Fargo and Buckshot discussed possible tactics for freeing the prisoners in that gulch. After a long silence Fargo said speculatively, "First we need to find out who the linchpin is. All criminal gangs depend on the one man who can control the group. And we need to separate the grain from the chaff. Besides the prisoners, there might be somebody in that hellhole willing to help us."

"Huh! You know me," Buckshot said. "I say we just free them prisoners and then burn that whole rat's nest down."

"I'm not asking for advice, jughead. Just thinking out loud. Still, maybe that's not such a bad idea. But like I said—there could be other innocents besides the ones locked up. The beauty in the tub, now she acted high and mighty. Maybe she *is* the linchpin. But the gal named Jasmine was taking orders. There could be more like her."

Buckshot started to reply when, abruptly, Fargo recognized

the Ovaro's trouble whicker coming from the rope corral. This was followed almost instantly by a shriek of pain. Fargo and Buckshot were the first to reach the corral followed by the rest of the men.

"Katy Christ," Buckshot said. "The hell you up to, Shoo Fly? You all right?"

Shoo Fly Jones lay doubled up in the grass clutching his crotch. A clear full moon showed his face twisted in pain.

"Fargo's horse . . . kicked me . . . in the nuts," he managed between hissing breaths.

"What in blazes were you doing behind his horse?" Big Ed demanded.

"And what's that knife for?" Fargo added, seeing it lying in the grass near Shoo Fly's hand. "Don't tell me you were trying to geld him?"

Looking sheepish, still grimacing, Shoo Fly managed to sit up. "I wasn't doing him no harm, Fargo, honest Injun. I was just trying to cut some hair from his tail."

"The hell for?"

"Ahh, you know . . . I wanted to weave it into little souvenir rings to sell to the men. I got some once from William Campbell's horse—you know, the famous Pony Express rider? Each ring fetched me a dollar."

Fargo, grinning and shaking his head, helped Shoo Fly to his feet. Buckshot joined the rest of them in a howl of mirth. "You tarnal fool! That's an uncut stallion, you ignut popinjay! You're lucky Fargo's Ovaro didn't cave your thick skull in."

Shoo Fly winced. "I'll be *lucky* if I ever sire a whelp. B'lieve me, I'm cured of the souvenir trade."

The rest of the men went back to their campfires, still roweling Shoo Fly, but Fargo and Buckshot lingered near the corral.

"Fargo, I ain't sleepy," Buckshot said. "You think our horses are rested up enough? They been grained good."

"I'm thinking the same thing you are—let's ride out tonight."

"Where we gonna start lookin' for this linchpin of yours?"

Fargo chuckled. "Where else? That limestone house. No use kidding each other—it's watching that little beauty and her pearls that has both of us in such a jo-fired hurry to get back."

"Yep," Buckshot admitted as they headed back to the camp circle to retrieve their saddles and weapons. "But there's a damn good chance we're playing the cobra to her mongoose."

8

Circling wide of the criminal nest in the gulch, Fargo and Buckshot arrived by midday at the same well-protected draw where they'd left their horses the night before last. They ate a meal of cold biscuits smeared with bacon grease, then slept until sundown.

They grained and watered the horses. As an extra precaution, they dug a shallow hole and lined it with Fargo's oilskin slicker before pouring water into it from the goatskin bag.

"In case we run into trouble," Fargo said, "they'll hold out all right for a few days, especially if it rains. We'll ground tether 'em loose so's they can pull out the pickets if they get desperate. Let's face it—if we're not back by that point, we'll likely be swinging from that gallows."

"Ain't *you* the sunny son of a bitch," Buckshot groused. "What about our long guns?"

"Let's leave them here. We might need them for a hot retreat. It'll be easier to move around in the gulch without them, and if we get into a shooting fray it'll likely be at close quarters. We've got plenty of ammo for our short guns. Besides, we'll have Patsy to persuade any pushy crowds."

"Yep. She likes to get her own way."

By now the lazy hard tails in the gulch were convinced they had run the two intruders off for good, and no sentries had been posted at the rim of the gulch. The two men were quickly in place at the western end overlooking the limestone house.

"Bathtub's been put up," Buckshot said, disappointment keen in his tone as he peered through the brush.

"Never mind. You expect a peep show every night? We'll scramble down and go in through that back door if we can.

Don't forget those two hombres armed like payroll guards. We want to avoid chucking lead if we can—the noise will bring the rest down on us like all wrath."

Both men found enough hand- and footholds to climb quickly down to the floor of the gulch in the generous light of a full moon. They shucked out their six-shooters. Fargo found the latchstring out and cautiously pushed the slab door open. The house had a narrow center hallway running its length with candles burning in brass wall sconces. Curtained archways opened off both sides. They could hear feminine voices conversing from the central room on the right.

Fargo nodded at Buckshot and they advanced on cat feet, Fargo wincing each time one of the floorboards creaked. They paused in front of the expensive damask curtains. Fargo recognized the musical lilt of the woman who had tantalized them during her erotic bath.

"I've assured you repeatedly, Jasmine, that the prisoners are not being abused. And certainly you are not. You're young and pretty, and I brought you to live with me for your protection, not so I'd have a servant. Your husband would still be alive if he had not foolishly resisted. Trying to pull a gun on a gang of armed men was certainly not the brightest decision of his life, was it? All of my men are under strict orders to avoid killing whenever possible."

"I've heard you give that order, Miss Lavoy, but I was there! Butch McDade is a liar! Jimmy had a gun, yes, but he never drew it. The moment Butch found it on him, he murdered him in cold blood."

"Well, I won't defend Butch. He'd shoot a nun for her gold tooth. He is mean and low and spiteful, the brooding kind that holds a grudge until it hollers for its mama. And I admit that most of the men in this gulch have oozed out of 'the pitch that defileth.' I am truly sorry about Jimmy. But right now the vermin in Hangtown are useful tools for me."

For me. Fargo glanced at Buckshot, who nodded to show he had heard. So that was the gait—everybody in the gulch was feeding at the same trough, and this was their linchpin, all right. Nor had either man missed the fateful word "Hangtown."

Fargo inserted the muzzle of his Colt between the overlapping curtains and began to nudge one aside. Suddenly he felt a blow like a mule kick to his head, saw a bright orange starburst, and his world shut down to black oblivion.

Fargo drifted in and out of patchy fog trying to claw his way back to the surface of awareness. He could hear voices, but not words. Finally his quivering eyelids twitched open.

His head throbbed like a Pawnee war drum, and when he tried to move, pain jolted through him. He was seated in a comfortable chair, his short gun, ammo belt, and Arkansas toothpick missing. The first thing he registered was a pleasant room featuring red plush furniture with fancy knotted fringes.

And then four sets of eyes watching him as if he were a piece of curiosa in a museum.

"Well," the brunette beauty greeted him, "Skye Fargo—a prince among knaves. Poor as Job's turkey but so utterly handsome."

There was a groan to his left as Buckshot began to regain awareness.

"You're both quite lucky," the brunette told Fargo in her musical voice. "El Burro and Norton are quite protective of me, and normally they would have decapitated you on the spot with their machetes. But I suspected you might be . . . visiting soon. So I gave them orders to simply incapacitate you so we might visit."

Wincing, Fargo sat up a little straighter. The pain in his head far surpassed his worst cheap-whiskey hangover.

"I do appreciate that, Miss Lavoy."

"So you know my name? May I inquire how you learned it?"

Fargo was still groggy, but not stupid enough to admit he had spied on her while she bathed. "Well, I heard this blond lass here call you Miss Lavoy. I don't know your front name."

"It's Jennifer although I prefer Jenny. The denizens of Hangtown have dubbed me Little Britches, a name I detest but tolerate. 'The Trailsman,' however, is a very fine nickname."

Fargo took her pleasing measure from the white columbine petals in her hair to the fancy side-lacing silk shoes.

"You look sweet as a scrubbed angel," he told her. "But I'd wager your halo is a bit tarnished."

"Be careful," she warned him. "You may have noticed the power balance is against you."

Buckshot groaned again and opened his eyes. The doe-eyed blonde named Jasmine watched Fargo with compassion and concern; in sharp contrast, El Burro and Norton seemed on the verge of eating his warm liver.

The pedestal table beside Fargo's chair held a big pottery bowl of water with rose petals floating in it. Jenny saw him staring at it.

"I like nice things," she informed him. "This furniture was stolen from a freight caravan. Sadly, some disappointed customer in Santa Fe will never receive his special order."

"We can't always get what we want," Fargo said philosophically.

"Oh, I plan to. This situation in Hangtown is merely a stepping-stone for me. You, however, seem to be in quite a pickle. Indeed, this may well turn out to be the end of the trail for a man who has travelled many."

"You might say fortune hasn't kissed me lately," he agreed, evoking a laugh from her.

"No one can fault your stoicism," she approved.

"I'm just curious," Fargo said. "Why did you expect me to be visiting?"

"Because most men run to type. Mr. Fargo, I know what manner of man you are said to be—and your celebrated skill at tracking. So when I learned that my unholy trinity, as I call my three uncouth lieutenants, had attacked your work crew and killed a man, it seemed a logical assumption that you would eventually find our little spa here in the gulch."

She paused before adding in a tone of naughty innuendo, "I knew that you would try to stick your oar in my boat, so to speak."

Fargo almost replied that he couldn't think of a nicer place to stick it. But El Burro had both hands on the butts of his Colt Navy revolvers and seemed to be praying for the slightest excuse to unlimber.

"You're right," Fargo said. "It was the attack that brought us down here."

"Who the hell took Patsy?" Buckshot interjected.

Jenny shifted her bewitching brown eyes to the speaker. "And who is your half-breed companion?"

"Buckshot Brady, ma'am," Buckshot replied. "Fargo likes to take me along so he won't die alone."

She studied him for a long moment. "Well, you're getting a bit long in the tooth. But you look well knit, and there's strong character in your face. If the famous Skye Fargo trusts you for dangerous work, that's a high recommendation indeed."

"Yeah, he's a pip," Buckshot said drily, shooting a murderous look at Fargo.

Jenny smiled at that, still watching him. "I heard all about the stand the two of you made, two days ago, against daunting odds. Yes indeed, I think both of you just might do . . ."

Buckshot brightened, jumping to conclusions. "Hell *yes*, we'll do! You and Jasmine both won't have no regrets."

She laughed again. "My stars! You're younger than you look."

"Just might do for what?" Fargo asked.

"Good help is extremely hard to find in an operation like mine, Mr. Fargo. You'll see what I mean in a few minutes. Norton, please go and fetch Butch McDade and his two companions."

The silent, unequivocally ugly bodyguard, the smaller of the two, nodded and left.

"You two are going to meet the three men who attacked you," Jenny Lavoy explained. "Their leader, and the second in command of this den of iniquity, is a raging bull named Butch McDade. He's a muscular, cruelly handsome bully of limited intellect, but very dangerous nonetheless. He's what is commonly called a gunslick—he has a lightning gun hand."

"And he's a common murderer!" Jasmine erupted. "He killed my husband in cold blood!"

Jenny ignored the emotional outburst. "There's also Waldo Tate, the human rodent. He's a cowardly back-shooter and spends much of his time in opium dreams. But he's quite cunning and provides the brain that McDade is missing. The third man, and the most dangerous in my estimation, is Lupe Cruz."

"Lupe Cruz?" Fargo interrupted. "I heard he was in these parts."

"So you know him?"

"I know of him. He's a blade-runner and rumored to be the best knife man that ever came out of Mexico. He hates *Tejanos* and he'll kill any man from the Panhandle without cause. After he kills them he cuts off their ears and wears them around his neck. He used to raid the old San Antonio Trail into Chihuahua until Texas Rangers ran him off."

"All true. He claims his sire was a grandee of Spain. But I happen to know that his scurvy-ridden father led a scalper army down in Sonora before he became a Comanchero slave trader in New Mexico Territory."

"Sounds to me," Fargo said, "like you keep some mighty unsavory company."

Jenny's dark eyes flashed indignation. "The phrase 'keeping company,' Mr. Fargo, is drifting close to an insult. Perhaps you'd like to revise that suggestive comment?"

She wore a dark calico skirt with a spanking-clean white shirtwaist. One hand dipped into a pocket of the skirt and emerged holding an over-and-under muff gun. It was aimed, Fargo noticed, at a spot he particularly cherished.

Sweat beaded on his scalp. "I misspoke, ma'am. I meant only that these men are on your payroll."

"That's better."

She raised her aim and Fargo flinched violently when the derringer barked, sending his hat spinning off his head.

"I hope that will teach you," she said demurely, "to remove your hat in the presence of a lady."

Buckshot quickly snatched off his cavalry hat.

Jenny nodded toward the massive mestizo. "This eternally silent gentleman is El Burro. He and Norton are my palace guard, and very effective at it. You see, they were both captured by Comanches. Their tongues were cut out and they were castrated. I rescued them in the desert and now they are intensely loyal—even Butch McDade and Lupe Cruz fear them. Not that either thug has anything to complain about—I

69

throw plenty of scraps to them. Their interest in me is more . . . carnal."

"I can understand that," Fargo said politely, picking up his hat and examining the new hole in it.

"It is a rare man," Jenny added, taking Fargo's measure with approving eyes, "who enjoys my favors."

"And a fortunate one, I'm sure," Fargo encouraged her.

She met his remark with a mysterious smile. "Sanctuary mucho, as they say in Spanglish. But don't presume on your good looks, Fargo. I'm a woman of . . . unconventional predilections."

She lost Fargo on that last word, but he decided to let it go. He could still feel the warm crease where her bullet had parted his hair, and her apparent fondness for "alterated" men had turned him cautious.

"Still," she added after studying him some more, "you just might come up to scratch. I certainly approve of what I've seen so far."

Fargo heard scuffing footsteps in the hallway.

"Here come my trusty retainers," Jenny said, her tone laced with sarcasm. "Don't believe what you hear me tell them about my plans for you two—I'll just be throwing a bone to the dogs."

"Why do you want me and Buckshot to meet them?" Fargo hurried to ask.

"Because soon," she replied, "I'm hoping you will kill them."

The curtains parted and Fargo got his first look at the trio that had set events in motion four days ago with their attack on the work crew.

Jenny had done a good job of describing them: Butch McDade with his trouble-seeking eyes and scornful twist of mouth; Waldo Tate with the pointy face of a rat and the bright, burning eyes of a consumptive; and Lupe Cruz with his disgusting human-ear necklace and dead, soulless eyes like two bone chips.

"What the . . . ?"

McDade's voice trailed off and his eyes went smoky with rage when he recognized the two men in the chairs.

"I'm not too impressed with your competence, Butch," Jenny teased him. "El Burro and Norton managed to do what you and half your men could not."

"The hell is this, Little Britches?" he demanded as if he had a right to know. "They here for tea and biscuits?"

McDade was the blustering type, Fargo realized, who had to work himself up to the kill. It was Cruz, more taciturn and calculating, he watched the closest. He wore leather *chivarra* trousers, a low shako hat, and a rawhide vest. But Fargo was most interested in the Spanish dag with a cord-wrapped hilt and a wide blade—spade shaped and perfectly balanced for the quick toss—that protruded from his boot.

"No need to rise on your hind legs, Butch," Jenny said in the soothing tone one uses with a dangerous horse. "I have a fertile mind when it comes to profiteering, and I assure you the situation is under control."

"Then why ain't these two cold as a wagon wheel? Them geldings of yours shoulda lopped off their heads by now."

"Everything in its own time."

Cruz saw Fargo watching him and flashed him a lips-only smile. "With *this* one, Senorita Lavoy," he advised, "the only good time is now."

"Nonsense, Lupe. He's stripped of his weapons and a prisoner in Hangtown. A man can't be more helpless than that—or more hopeless."

McDade grunted and shifted his glance to Buckshot. "Who's this piece of half-breed shit?"

"Ask your mother," Buckshot piped up. "She knows me real good."

McDade snarled and crossed toward Buckshot's chair, right hand balling into a fist. Fargo shot one long leg out and tripped him. McDade crashed heavily to the floor. He sprang up cursing, but as he reached for the walnut-gripped Remington in his tied-down holster, loud, menacing clicks stopped him. El Burro and Norton held all four of the Colts aimed at him.

"This is not the Bucket of Blood," Jenny scolded him as if he were a rambunctious schoolboy. "There'll be no clash-of-stags roughhousing in my home."

"What is this shit?" McDade demanded. "You're the one

said Fargo would dance on air if he was fool enough to enter Hangtown. Now here you are—putting *me* under the gun!"

"Miss Lavoy," Fargo spoke up, "you must have dredged mighty deep to come up with this sweet outfit."

Cruz grinned while McDade flushed with anger from his neck to his scalp. "You don't come into this gulch swinging your eggs, buckskins!"

"Butch is right, Mr. Fargo," Jenny warned. "Remember that power balance I warned you about. Right now your life is hanging by a thread."

She looked at McDade again. "I'm not protecting Fargo, Butch. I'm protecting a valuable asset."

"I don't savvy."

"Yes, you generally don't. Did you yourself not call Fargo a newspaper darling?"

"Sure, on account he is. You'd think he was ten inches taller than God, the way they gush over him."

Jenny nodded. "You're making my argument for me. Wouldn't you agree that Skye Fargo stories are good for newspaper circulation? And wouldn't you also agree that the merchant capitalists who own the newspapers want to make money?"

"Hell, who don't?"

"Exactly. Imagine millions of readers back east eagerly following the story about how a group of powerful, influential newspapers have agreed to pay a ransom to free their darling. A ransom of, say, ten thousand dollars—a paltry sum to them but a windfall for us."

McDade pulled on the point of his chin as her point sank home. Waldo Tate—McDade's missing brain, according to Jenny—spoke up for the first time. Fargo noticed that an ugly carbuncle bulged one side of his neck.

"Little Britches is right, Butch. That ten thousand would earn the crapsheets ten times that much in profits. It's smart business for them."

"Maybe it would be at that," he admitted. "But they ain't like the families we're shaking down. They'll want proof Fargo is alive so they don't look like fools if they're hornswoggled."

"And we'll give it to them," Jenny said. "We invite a

photographer to meet us at someplace well away from here. He takes the photograph of Fargo back east and they deliver our money."

"Now just hold your horses," Butch said. "You mean we actually *give* them Fargo after we're paid?"

"Don't be dense. A dog returns to his own vomit, and Fargo will likewise come after us again. We'll kill our bearded visitor *and* whoever delivers the ransom. There's no effective law out here, and there's a very nasty war on now— that means no military posse."

Don't believe what you hear me tell them—I'll just be throwing a bone to the dogs. Jenny's words from just a few minutes ago, Fargo realized, were as reliable as a wildcat bank. She probably did want him and Buckshot to eventually kill this "unholy trinity" as she called them—she knew out-law men well enough to know they would sull at some point, raping and killing her. And why risk the lives of her loyal bodyguards in the effort to stop them?

But clearly she was a master at working both sides of the fence, and Fargo suspected she also intended to go through with the ransom plan. And she would indeed kill Fargo rather than hand him over and have to tangle with him again.

"Well, it ain't the worst plan I ever heard," Butch finally conceded.

"Good," Jenny said. "We'll work out the fine details later."

"On your feet," McDade ordered Fargo. "And don't get cute on me. You too, 'breed."

"Just what are you doing?" Jenny demanded.

"Wha'd'ya think? Taking them over to the guardhouse with the rest of the prisoners."

Jenny shook her pretty head. "Out of the question. You and your . . . men will get drunk and kill them. They will be kept under guard here. I have hidden their weapons, and El Burro and Norton are fully capable of controlling them."

Butch's jaw slacked open. "Lady, are you shittin' me?"

"I told you he's a valuable asset."

Fargo watched Butch and Cruz exchange a long look, two curs watching the new dog in town mount their bitch. "I'll just bet he is," Butch replied, his voice heavy with sarcasm and jealous resentment.

But when El Burro parted the curtains for them, all three sullen-faced men filed out.

"Well, boys," Jenny said to Fargo and Buckshot, rubbing her palms briskly together to express her exuberance, "it looks like the fun is just beginning."

9

Fargo and Buckshot were fed bowls of stew and then led into a nearly empty, windowless room right across the hall from the room where Norton and Burro slept. Jasmine had prepared two sleeping pallets for them and left a squat candle and a greasy deck of cards on an upended packing crate, the only "furnishings."

"Mr. Fargo," Jenny said from the arched doorway, "your reputation for hairbreadth escapes has preceded you. But either Norton or El Burro will be sitting in the hallway at all times. You'll catch a weasel asleep before you surprise them. If either of you so much as pokes his nose into the hall, you will be shot dead and strung up on the gallows. I trust that's clearly understood?"

Fargo glanced up into El Burro's clay-mask face and implacable eyes. The mestizo's left hand—the one not filled with blue steel—stroked the sisal scabbard of his machete.

"You have a knack for making your terms very clear," Fargo replied diplomatically.

"Good. If you gents behave yourselves, we may come to terms more agreeable to you. Mr. Brady, are you familiar with mahjong?"

"Ma Jong? I ain't never heard of the lady."

Jenny tossed back her head and laughed, revealing a lovely throat smooth as ivory. "It's not a person, you benighted savage. It's a Chinese game. Usually four persons play it, but later tonight I'll send for you and teach you the game."

"Christmas crackers!" Buckshot exclaimed when the two men were alone. "She's gonna send for me, Skye! You don't think—"

"No, I don't." Fargo cut him off. "She's up to something though."

"Huh. You're just jealous 'cause she picked me first for the old slap 'n' tickle. You heard her say there was character in my face."

"And rocks in your head. Keep your damn voice down, wouldja? Those 'palace guards' of hers can't talk, but they can sure hear. And never mind the damn frippet—we gotta figure out how to wangle out of this deal without getting our wicks snuffed."

Fargo was already examining the whitewashed side wall, but it seemed solid as a revetment. He sniffed the air. "You can still smell castor oil. This room was used to store packs of beaver pelts, all right."

"Speaking of beaver—that Jenny is silky-satin, sure enough," Buckshot said. "But holy Christ! She makes Tammany politics look like Sunday school. The hell's she up to, Skye?"

"I've never learned to read sign on the breast of a normal woman let alone a scheming hellcat like her. One thing's certain sure: we need to clap the stopper on her."

Fargo's tobacco hadn't been taken. He lit one of his skinny Mexican cigars in the candle flame. "We can't count on our horses staying put forever. And if we lose them, we lose our rifles—the only weapons we got left unless we find our short guns."

"Them sons-a-bitches took Patsy," Buckshot snarled. "Skye, the *hell* is that pert skirt doing? First she tells us she wants us to kill them three sage rats for her. Then she tells them we're gonna be ransomed and kilt."

"It's a stumper. My guess is she's hedging her bets. It could be she does want us to kill those 'lieutenants' of hers because she's smart enough to know that she's dancing on dynamite if she lets them live much longer. But this ransom deal—it was worked out too careful in her mind to just be a spur-of-the-moment lie."

"Yeah, that shines, don't it?" Buckshot agreed. "That business just now about how her and us might come to 'more agreeable terms'—you think mebbe she's got us in mind to replace them other three as her top dirt workers?"

"Yeah, I thought about that. It could be. A woman that beautiful is used to turning men into her lap dogs. If that's her drift, we need to play along."

"What's your size-up on McDade and them other two sidewinders?"

"Butch is a hothead and a bully, and according to Jenny he's a quick-draw artist, which makes him dangerous. Waldo Tate is only a threat if you turn your back to him. But I'll warn you right now, old son—*don't* underrate that Mexer or he'll cut you to trap bait in a heartbeat. His six-gun's just for show. It's his blade that kills."

"Mister, we're rowed *way* the hell up Salt River," Buckshot said. "No horses, no guns or ammo, and it ain't just these two bodyguards and them three snake-shits we gotta fret—this whole cockchafin' gulch is filled with hard cases licking Jenny's hand. And it'd be easier to tie down a bobcat with a piece of string than to figger her out."

"'Fraid so," Fargo agreed. "She's holding a candle for the devil, all right. Matter fact, she might even be his mistress."

The two men sat on their pallets and played five-card draw for the next hour or so while they tried—fruitlessly—to figure a plan of action. Now and then El Burro or Norton poked his head in to check on them.

"Both them dickless bastards give me the fidgets," Buckshot said. "They're itchin' for a chance to point our toes to the sky."

Fargo nodded, slapping down a card. "They're more dangerous than Butch and those other two."

The next time the curtains parted, however, Jasmine stepped into the room with El Burro behind her.

"Mr. Brady," she said, "Miss Lavoy wants to play mahjong now."

Buckshot sent Fargo a smug look as he scrambled to his feet. "If she wants to play, I'm her man. Looks like you gotta play solitaire now, Trailsman. Keep your chin up—might be your turn next."

Fargo was pleasantly surprised when Jasmine remained behind after Buckshot was herded off at gunpoint.

She sent him a tentative smile. "I'm afraid your friend has the wrong idea."

"Wrong ideas are his trademark," Fargo replied, adding, "I didn't know I was allowed visitors."

"I'm not exactly a visitor," she admitted. "I was ordered to come here."

"Oh." Fargo's soaring expectations took a sudden nose-dive. With him it was always the woman's choice. "Why?" he added.

"She . . . well, she said she wants a 'full report' on you."

Fargo studied the pretty girl in the dancing candlelight. She was barefoot and wore a yellow gingham dress that showcased her narrow waist and flaring hips. Her hair was a spun-gold waterfall tumbling in waves over her shoulders. Even in this soft lighting her eyes were a sparkling emerald green. It had been far too long since Fargo had been with a woman, and heat stirred in his loins like the tickling brush of wing tips.

"What kind of report?" he pressed her.

"Mainly, she told me, on your . . . 'prowess in the sack,' I think she put it."

"She should find out for herself instead of ordering you to do it. C'mon in and sit down."

"That Jenny Lavoy is—well, she's not quite right in her upper story," Jasmine said as she folded down onto the pallet beside Fargo and smoothed her dress with both hands.

"You mean she's insane?"

"No, not exactly that, I don't s'pose. She's very intelligent and she don't seem to do crazy sorta things. But there's stuff she tells me—you know, about men and bedroom matters?—that would make a horse blush. She's not interested in doing things the normal way that men and women do them."

This intelligence intrigued Fargo. "I don't mean to embarrass you, Jasmine, but could you chew that a little finer?"

"Well . . . see, she's got this strange book with pictures of men and women, you know, doing it. But some of the things they're up to—why, it's hard to imagine how anybody even thought them up. Not that some of them ain't, you know, exciting. There's this one . . . well, I'd rather not say. But I think she's got you in mind for trying it, Mr. Fargo."

"Skye," he corrected her, even more intrigued but unwilling to put her on the spot. "So you're a prisoner just like me?"

"Not exactly like you. I can wander around the house and go out in the yard. I cook and wash for her and them two freakish bodyguards. She's holding me for ransom from my folks back in Iowa. There's five other prisoners down in the gulch. She don't treat me too bad, Mr. Far—I mean, Skye. But I don't believe for one blessed minute that she plans to let any of us live."

"That's my read on her, too," Fargo said. "And that means none of us has a damn thing to lose by trying to escape."

"I'll try to help if I can. But I'm all at sea about what to do. She's already told me I'll be killed the first time I break her rules. That is, I'll be killed after all them men in the gulch have their use of me first."

"Don't stick your neck out. But keep your eyes and ears open and try to learn what they did with our weapons."

Jasmine's shoulder was touching Fargo's arm, and the clean woman smell of her tantalized him like hell thirst. He made an effort to even out his breathing. He said, "I heard you and her talking about how Butch McDade killed your husband."

"Yes, I'm a widow at twenty-three. Me and Jim left Ohio to join my brother and his wife in Oregon to start a lumber mill. We didn't have the money to outfit for a wagon train, but there was new Overland and Butterfield stage routes. We saved up for two stagecoach tickets—laws, they was expensive—but McDade and his bunch jumped us west of Fort Laramie."

It felt, to a hopeful Fargo, like Jasmine was leaning against him more.

"Skye?"

"Hmm?"

"I know it must sound shameless, me being a new widow and all. But I was glad when Miss Lavoy sent me in here. As soon as I saw you today, I felt the man hunger in me. See, me and Jim used to do it all the time—sometimes all night long. And I got use to wanting it all the time. I got nothing on under my dress."

"That's all I need to hear," Fargo said.

Her dress looped up the front. Fargo opened the bodice and eagerly cupped her firm loaves. The nipples instantly stiffened against his palms.

"Mine ain't as big as Jenny Lavoy's," she said low in his ear, her breath warm and soft on his face and neck. "But I ain't no member of the itty-bitty titty club, neither."

"They're perfect," Fargo assured her, bending down to suck and nibble first one, then the other. The hard but pliant nipples were like mint-flavored gumdrops in his mouth.

After only a minute of this they were both panting like dogs in August. Fargo stretched her out on the pallet and pushed the dress up and over her hips. Her blond bush was soft as corn silk. She opened her thighs wide, egging Fargo on as she revealed the nooks, crannies, and chamois-soft folds of her sex.

"Skye, I'm hot as a branding iron," she said, her tone pleading.

Fargo knew the feeling well after his long erotic drought. On his knees between her straddled legs, he dropped his buckskin trousers. His blue-veiner was iron hard and leaped with each heartbeat that sent hot blood surging into it.

Her emerald eyes widened at the sight of it. "Oh, my lands! I ain't seen too many peeders, but—but I didn't know they got that big."

"Don't forget, hon—it's angry right now, and it's you making it big. Now let's take care of this."

The inside of her thighs were glistening with her desire. Fargo slipped both hands under her taut butt and adjusted her to the perfect angle. He nudged just his purple-swollen tip into her nether portal and rubbed it rapidly back and forth on her clitty until she shivered and writhed at the cascading waves of pleasure.

"*All* of it!" she begged. "Fill me up with it!"

One flex of his ass sent Fargo's shaft sinking deep, parting the tight but flexible walls of her cunny like water before a ship's prow. Both of them gasped at the explosive pleasure, greater than any other Fargo knew, that engulfed them in mindless, wordless, animal ecstasy.

"Hard, Skye!" the little vixen encouraged him, her words a husky moan. "Give it to me hard and fast!"

Her words were fuel to the fire as Fargo turned into a piston of pleasure, driving in and out in a frenzy of lust that scootched the pallet across the floor. Whimpering and crying out, she locked her slender, shapely legs behind his back and flexed her love muscle over and over, amplifying his pleasure and encouraging Fargo to long, hard, fast strokes until hell wouldn't have it again.

Once, twice, a third time she cried out as repeated climaxes drove her to the brink of passing out from pleasure overload. Fargo held off as long as possible until the hot, tingling tickle in his groin erupted like a howitzer blast. His reservoir of pent-up lust was so great that he needed at least a dozen after-spasms to spend himself.

They both collapsed, their breathing ragged and uneven for a full minute. It was even longer before their mindless daze slowly wore off like a drug.

"I ain't never had it like that, Skye," she finally managed. "I'm gonna be sore for a while, but it'll be a *nice* kind of sore."

"And now you make your report to Jenny."

"I'll tell the truth, but I can tell you right now she won't believe it. No woman would."

The dilapidated clapboard shack in the middle of Hangtown was a far cry from Jenny Lavoy's comfortable home at the far end of the gulch. It had a rammed-earth floor with an old Franklin stove hunkering in the middle of the only room. A skunk-oil lamp with a rag wick sat atop a table made from a wagon tailgate nailed to two sawhorses. Three crude shakedowns crawling with cockroaches completed the furnishings.

Butch McDade sat at the table, his face dour as he poured himself another jolt glass of red-eye and tossed it back fast. Then he slammed the glass back to the table.

"Shit, piss, and corruption!" he growled. "See how it is, Lupe? That's Skye Fargo, the biggest pussy hound in the West, up there right now with *our* meat!"

Lupe Cruz, occupied in running a whetstone over the Toledo steel of his blade, nodded. "This Fargo, he could seduce a Vestal Virgin, uh?"

"Just the other night," McDade fumed, "she was telling me and you how she was close to picking one of us for her reg'lar night man. Then that strutting peacock Fargo has to ruin the whole shivaree. Somehow we *got* to get shut of that lanky bastard."

Waldo Tate sat on his shakedown, nervously snapping the wheel of one spur with his finger. Butch slammed his fist into the table so hard that the whiskey bottle jumped.

"Blast you, Waldo! Leave that fuckin' spur alone or I'll ram it down your gullet! God*damn* you are a nervous son of a bitch."

"I need me a pipe, is all."

"Never mind them tar balls. You're the one with the good think piece on him. How do we get Fargo outta that house and locked up in the guardhouse with the others before he takes Little Britches *and* Jasmine from us?"

Waldo shook his head in disgust. "Butch, you're tough as a two-bit steak, but you don't know from nothing where Jenny is concerned."

"The hell you mean?"

"Why'n't you quit hot-jawing about poon for a minute and think about the *real* danger Fargo represents?"

"You got a chicken bone caught in your throat? Speak your piece."

Waldo stood up and began nervously circling the shack like a puma on the prowl. "That story she fed us about ransoming Fargo and then killing him and going equal shares with us—did you swallow it?"

"Hell, *you* did. You said it was a good plan."

Waldo shook his head impatiently. "I had to, Butch. You were standing there raising a stink, and both them body-guards had their barking irons out. I was scared she'd order them to burn us down on the spot."

"Well, why *ain't* it a good plan?"

"Butch, do you need it carved on wood and shoved up your ass? Don't you take my drift? She might go through with the ransom plan, all right—that bitch doesn't miss a trick where profit is concerned. But she doesn't have to kill Fargo. She might have bigger plans for him."

Lupe Cruz, quicker on the mental trigger than Butch, suddenly stopped honing his blade and watched Waldo intently.

"Damn you, Waldo," Butch said in a low, dangerous voice, "either you quit taking the long way around the barn or I irrigate your guts."

"I'm telling you there's at least an even chance she means to deal Fargo in and have him kill *us*. Butch, that little hussy could sell a six-gun to a Quaker, and Fargo is no psalm-singer. Christ, he's a hard killer and tough as boar bristles. Do you know any man who would turn down top-shelf quiff *and* easy money?"

Butch poured himself another jolt but forgot to drink it as he mulled Waldo's words. "So you think that's what's on the spit? She means to throw in with Fargo and haze us out? Kill us, even?"

"No," Waldo corrected him. "I said there's an even chance. How can you tell with Little Britches?"

"She's a *ladina*," Lupe put in. "A sly one. So is Fargo. The two of them together, *ay Caramba!*"

Butch frowned. "I don't like to shit where I eat. So far Little Britches has been generous in splitting up the swag."

"She's not the problem," Waldo insisted. "It's Fargo coming to Hangtown that upset the cart, right? Lupe's right— Little Britches is a sly bitch, but without Fargo to give her ideas, she'll have to string along with us. She's got nobody else, and without us to control them, the rest of the men would be all over her like white on rice."

McDade slowly nodded, seeing the truth of this. "Yeah. The rest of the men in Hangtown ain't worth a cup of cold piss without us to control 'em."

"Now you're snapping wise," Waldo approved. "That bitch has a mind like a steel trap, but she's still only a woman."

"So you see how it is, boys," McDade said. "Never mind saving Fargo for any ransom plan—as quick as we can, we got to close his account for good."

10

Fargo, worn out after his pleasant interlude with Jasmine, was just entering the Land of Nod when a hot string of curses jolted him awake.

"The hell's your beef?" he snapped at Buckshot, who had just returned to the room.

"That crazy, highfalutin bitch, that's what. And me thinking she wanted to play bury the picket pin."

Fargo chuckled. "There's a saying among poker players: If you look around the table and can't find the chump, it's probably you."

"Sing it, brother. All she done was prod me with questions mostly 'bout you. That high-hatting little bitch."

Fargo rose up on one elbow. "Keep your voice down. What questions?"

"Was you really a 'knight in buckskins' like some of them ink slingers say. Did you ever break the law, do you bitch about being poor, do you ever talk 'bout what you'd do if you ever come into money, have you ever outright murdered anybody, shit like that."

"Hunh. How'd you play it?"

Buckshot yanked his boots off, still muttering curses. "Just like me and you planned it. I told her the newspaper stories was swamp gas. I said me and you done some smuggling and how we sold guns to warpath Injins and such. And if she asks you, you gunned down a sheriff in Arkansas after he caught you selling whiskey to Choctaws."

"Sounds like you laid it on pretty thick, hoss."

"At least pre*tend* I ain't a soft brain. I told her the sheriff was crooked as cat shit, and how you was mostly a straight arrow but now and then you got bucked off the straight and narrow path when temptation got the best of you—'specially when a comely lass was in the mix."

"Well, she's mighty sharp," Fargo said. "Maybe she saw right through you and maybe she didn't. Anyhow, it's a good sign for us that she asked all those questions—sounds like she's thinking about cutting us into her operation. Or maybe it was all a smoke screen just to keep us guessing. Did she feel you out, too?"

"Yup. Asked me flat out if I was tired of the penny-ante game. I told her I was like most men drifting around the West—willing to do most anything if it wouldn't get me jugged or hanged."

"Sounds like you played the best hand you could. But we can't look too eager to throw in with her—we have to let her nudge us a little, make her think we'll fall, all right, but only with a little push."

Buckshot suddenly sniffed the air. "Damn your bones, Fargo! I wunnered where Jasmine disappeared to. You trimmed her while I was dickin' around with them little Chinee tiles—I can smell the woman scent."

Fargo grinned. "If a ripe apple falls off the tree, I eat it."

"Uh-huh. Was the apple any good?"

"Never mind that. Any idea where our weapons might be?"

"I looked around best I could but couldn't see no hiding places. I'd wager them two dickless yacks got 'em somewheres in their room."

"Distinct possibility," Fargo agreed. "Now get some shut-eye. I got a hunch we're gonna need it."

With no window in the room Fargo had no idea what time it was when El Burro kicked him awake.

Both men pulled on their boots and, with the two bodyguards watching them at gunpoint, they were led to a rickety jakes behind the house where they relieved themselves. Fargo saw that the day's new sun was just then peeking over the eastern horizon. Then they were led back inside to a small but tidy kitchen where Jenny Lavoy sat at a cloth-covered table drinking tea.

"Good morning, my rustic houseguests," she greeted them cheerfully. "Jasmine, heap their plates—Fargo, especially, must be *very* hungry."

Jasmine, standing before an iron cookstove, smiled over her shoulder at Fargo. She served up plates of hash and biscuits.

"Tell me, Mr. Fargo," Jenny said as the two men tied into their food, "have you ever been to San Francisco?"

Fargo nodded. "I knew the place when some still called it Yerba Buena. For my money it's the roughest city in the West."

"Nonsense. True, the Barbary Coast and areas along the Embarcadero are unsavory and full of rattle and hullabaloo. But there is a great deal of money and some fine mansions up in the hills. I used to cut quite a swath there."

Fargo studied her across the table. She looked striking— even angelic—in a white linen dress, her hair neatly coifed in braids under a jeweled silver tiara.

"I can believe that," he assured her. "And, yet, now you're stuck in a pukehole called Hangtown. From president to postman, huh?"

The smile she gave him was bright but strained. "Stuck? Not at all. Yes, I suffered a . . . reversal of fortunes in San Francisco, true. But Hangtown is a means, not an end. It is merely phase one in my plan—the phase that takes me from dirty money to clean, from the abject squalor here to the purposeless splendor I will once again enjoy in San Francisco."

"Purposeless splendor?" Fargo repeated dubiously.

"Yes, a hallmark of the fabulously wealthy. And it will begin with a beautiful marble villa featuring a sunken Italian garden."

Fargo nodded politely. "Sounds real nice."

She laughed, sweet, tinkling notes. "I take your skepticism for granted. But I hope to overcome it—for your sake *and* mine. And you might be surprised at just how nicely phase one is developing. Even in this 'pukehole,' as you call it, I've got a gown of organdy and tulle shipped all the way from Paris. I've got a hat that would cost you a year's wages. I have a chemise embroidered with fine lace that—"

"All them fancy feathers," Buckshot cut her off, still

rankled about last night's disappointment and fed up with this woman's foolish talk, "don't mean spit to a man. All we want is to see pretty gals naked."

Her cold stare at Buckshot was a clear warning. "Yes, and the damned want ice water in hell, too, do they not? Speak over me like that again, Mr. Brady, and I'll have El Burro bore a hole through your tongue."

"Yes, ma'am," he said meekly, wiping his plate clean with a biscuit.

"Now that you're both finished eating," she said briskly, standing up, "it's time for a bit of unpleasant but necessary business. Norton, the ropes, please. If you gentlemen will follow me outside . . ."

Fargo and Buckshot exchanged uncomfortable glances at the ominous word "ropes." In a place called Hangtown, the word resonated with sinister force. Everybody except Jasmine filed outside, Jenny blithely chirping as if she were explaining the fine points of ikebana.

"By now, gentlemen, Butch McDade and his cronies will be in a fine pucker after discussing the events of last night. They will, of course, have serious doubts about my honesty and true motives." She smiled sweetly at Fargo, a gorgeous angel on Satan's payroll. "Can you imagine that?"

"It's hard to feature," Fargo said from a deadpan as her two loyal henchmen tied the prisoners' hands behind their backs.

"Isn't it, though? But as I was saying, the unholy trinity will doubt me and spread the word throughout Hangtown that their mayor is mollycoddling two dangerous enemies. We must put the crusher on that rumor immediately by giving both of you a little tour of our thriving settlement. That way all of them will see the evidence that you are hardly my favorites—which, by the way, you certainly are."

She turned to El Burro and Norton and gave them instructions in a tone implying she was teaching children to buckle their shoes. "Now, boys, I want plenty of blood and bruising, but *no* permanent damage. And for goodness' sakes, Burro, nothing like the blow you gave Boots Winkler. Don't damage Mr. Fargo's marvelous teeth, and Mr. Brady can hardly afford to lose any more."

"Don't break my glass eye, neither," Buckshot quickly interposed.

Jenny studied his face closely. "My goodness, it is glass! I thought you were just walleyed. Yes, Norton, spare the glass eye."

"Look here," Fargo protested. "This—"

He swallowed the rest of the sentence when El Burro gave him a paster in the face that almost knocked Fargo out of his boots. He was still doing the Virginia reel backward when the slab-faced mestizo waded into him, delivering two short, hard jabs, one to each of Fargo's eyes. When Fargo's knees buckled, El Burro picked him up as easily as a sack of feathers and punched him in the nose—not hard enough to break it but sufficient to send blood spraying.

He finished off with a fast, hard series of slaps to Fargo's lips, splitting them open on his teeth. Fargo could hear the sickening thuds and painful grunts as Norton gave Buckshot the same treatment.

"That's fine," Jenny announced cheerfully. "Lift up their shirts and smear some of the blood on those, too. Leave their hands tied, of course—they are, after all, prisoners. Come along, everyone, let's stroll through the gulch."

"Ma'am," Buckshot managed, "if me and Fargo are your favorites, I'd hate like hell to be in your bad books."

Fargo, feeling woozy and unsteady on his feet, cast a baleful eye at El Burro. He spat out a gob of blood and said, "You know—I felt sorry for you two when Jenny described what the Comanches did to you. But there are limits to human sympathy, and you just reached mine."

"Why, Mr. Fargo!" Jenny exclaimed, clearly amused. "Are you threatening Burro?"

"I don't make threats," Fargo replied in the same mild tone. "I'm just telling him he'd better kill me because I'm sure-God gonna kill him."

At least, Fargo noted gratefully as Jenny led her odd-looking troupe into the gulch, it had rained during the night—he could see fresh puddles pockmarking the hog wallow that passed for Hangtown's only street. That meant the little cistern he and Buckshot had made for their horses had been replenished somewhat. He only hoped the tethers were long enough to allow them enough graze to keep them in the draw.

But if the two men didn't escape this place soon, Fargo realized, they'd lose both their horses and their rifles—and likely their lives.

Jenny took Fargo's elbow and pushed him slightly ahead of the others, speaking low so only he could hear.

"You know, Jasmine must be the excitable and melodramatic type. She gave me a rather incredible report about you last night."

"Oh? How so?"

"I'm not saying she lied to me, mind you. But her experience with men is probably limited to her late husband. Her description of your . . . male endowment has to be gross exaggeration. Fisherman's lie and all that?"

She gave him a quizzical glance.

"Distinct possibility," Fargo agreed. "The light was dim."

"Hmm. As to her rapturous account of your supposed prowess and endurance, well, I'm told each horse bucks to its own pattern, but so far as I can tell men are all the same. Sixty-second wonders . . . and the handsome ones like you are the most disappointing. One quick grunt and they fall asleep."

Fargo shrugged. "Best way to check the weather," he advised, "is to step outside into it."

"I've got a plan," she said mysteriously. "But a sexually conventional man will not do."

She left it there, so Fargo said, "This gulch is full of woman-starved men. They can't all be conventional."

"You'd have to know my unique tastes to be sure of that. Besides, you can see the lice leaping off their filthy clothes. That's why Butch . . . gathered up some soiled doves to sate the brutes. Unfortunately, the girls were barbarously treated and made their escape."

"Leaving you and the prisoners the only women in town?"

"Sadly, yes. If things come to a head, I'm afraid I may have to offer up Jasmine as a sacrifice. As for me, I'd rather wallow with hogs."

"Yeah, but do you tell them that? Or do you keep them all het up so they'll do your bidding?"

She scowled darkly. "I'll thank you to keep your nose out of the pie."

A moment later, however, she smiled. "Maybe that was the wrong metaphor?"

Fargo grinned. "I sure hope not."

Hangtown looked far more squalid and disgusting in the stark light of day. Rats nearly the size of rabbits feasted on the garbage strewn everywhere. The slapdash hovels and she-bangs made the poorest farmer's chicken coop look like Buckingham Palace.

Jenny made a point of starting her "tour" at the far end by the gallows. The freshest of the corpses was covered in a shifting blanket of bluebottle flies and the putrid stench of death—sickly sweet and heavy—tickled Fargo's gag reflex.

Jenny held a lace-edged handkerchief over her nose. "It's sickening, I know, but it's the smell of money."

Fargo looked at Buckshot and shook his head in amazement. Jenny caught the gesture and laughed. "There ought to be a law, right, Mr. Fargo?"

As they headed back into the gulch she pointed to a shack near the center of the outlaw outpost. "That's the place shared by Butch McDade, Lupe Cruz, and Waldo Tate—just in case you ever need to know."

Again Fargo exchanged a quick glance with Buckshot, raising his eyebrows in curiosity. That remark, Fargo reflected, sounded like an invitation to kill her "unholy trinity." But with this odd woman, motives were something written on water.

Two large army tents sat opposite each other. She led them into the one on the north side of the hog wallow.

"We call this," she explained, "the Temple of Morpheus. Neither gospel nor gunpowder will ever reform Hangtown, so I made sure there's a brake on men's wilder impulses."

The place reeked of opium and many of the "patrons" were slumped over tables asleep or sat with their eyes glazed in trances. Fargo spotted Waldo Tate watching them serenely from eyes like dull glass orbs.

"I detest opiates myself," she confided to her prisoners. "But even a benevolent tyrant is wise to keep her subjects . . . subdued as much as possible. Liquor makes men wild, so I make sure the bartenders 'baptize' it by watering it down for most of the men. Do you use the Chinese pipe, Mr. Fargo?"

He shook his head. "I've made my share of enemies, and for me the readiness is all."

"The readiness is all," she repeated in an admiring tone. "What a felicitous phrase. My sentiments exactly. Perhaps we shall see which one of us most lives up to that credo?"

"Judging from the condition of my face," Fargo replied, "I'd say you've got the edge on me."

She led them back outside. By now the few men in the street had spotted her little group and warily followed as Jenny aimed for the other big tent across the street.

"Good," she said in a satisfied tone. "They've seen my battered and bloodied prisoners. Now we'll add the crowning touch and take you into our mean facsimile of a saloon, the Bucket of Blood."

"You promised a complete tour," Fargo spoke up. "So what about that place?"

He pointed with his chin toward the crude stone structure with a guard seated out front.

She sent him a canny look. "I see you know all about our . . . guests? By all means, let's look in on them."

"Morning, Little Britches," the guard greeted her, doffing his hat. He glanced at Fargo and Buckshot and whistled sharply. "Man alive! These two b'hoys have been chawed up something fierce."

Jenny led them into the dim, dank-smelling interior. Fargo spotted four dejected, hopeless-looking adults, a young couple and a middle-aged couple. They sat on filthy straw pallets, the young woman clutching an infant. Their clothing was dirty and rumpled, the air stale and foul; roaches and flies crawled everywhere, and the young mother kept brushing them from her baby's filthy blanket.

"Not ideal conditions," Jenny admitted, "but they're fed regularly and get clean water."

"Please, miss," the young mother pleaded, "my little girl needs milk. She can't hold down the solid food."

"I'm truly sorry," Jenny replied, "but we have no cows in Hangtown. Perhaps a little cornmeal mush will help—I'll see that you get some. As soon as we receive the ransom—I mean, the travel funds—you'll be free to go."

The desperate young woman gave Fargo a pleading look that knifed him to his core. He felt a hot welling of anger at the sight of the pale, sickly child, but he guessed he was being tested and held his face expressionless. Jenny's questioning of Buckshot last night suggested she had a partnership in mind, an idea Fargo had to encourage.

Back outside in the bright morning sunlight, Jenny looked at Fargo and demanded, "Well? In the parlance of the frontier, was that too rich for your belly?"

Fargo lifted a shoulder, clamping his teeth around his first retort. He had to walk a fine line here because this woman had a potent mind. He needed to come off as reluctant but flexible.

"You don't really plan to turn them loose, do you?"

"How can I? They know too much."

"Well, I don't care too much about the men, Miss Lavoy. But kidnapping and murdering women and children doesn't set too well with me."

"It's not my first choice, Mr. Fargo, but they bring in the most money."

"Yeah, I guess that makes sense. But kidnapping is too risky for the profit. If the crapsheets get into a boil over it, you could have a smart chance of trouble on your hands. There's quicker, easier ways to make a lot more money without all the national outrage."

"Such as . . . ?"

"Well, like heisting mining company payrolls. There's several big operations just south of here in the Front Range. They usually have a light guard, and the public doesn't give a damn if the big bugs in silk toppers get robbed."

She watched Fargo with keen interest. "I see. Have you ever robbed one?"

"No, but I've been sorely tempted."

By now they had stepped into the smoky, stinking interior of the Bucket of Blood. Fargo realized most of the denizens of Hangtown were here, packed in like maggots in cheese—perhaps thirty men. They included Butch McDade and Lupe Cruz, leaning against the plank bar while they exercised their livers.

"Well, now," an obviously pleased McDade said, looking at the battered and swollen maps of the two prisoners. "This is more like it. Why'n't you just have them two geldings of yours finish the job, Little Britches? Better yet, let Lupe here slit their entrails open."

"They're money in our pockets, Butch, so long as they're alive."

A big, florid-faced bully wearing a filthy shirt sewn from old feed sacks moved in closer, lips twisted in scorn as he studied Fargo. "So this here's the big crusader, huh? The big man, brought down by a little chit of a girl no bigger'n a minute. Pull up your skirt, Nancy, and try to look brave."

Laughter and jeers exploded throughout the tent.

"And glom this half-breed gazabo siding him," the loud-mouth taunted. "Why, they must be a couple of them gal-boys you hear tell of. Tell me, Fargo, which one pitches and which one catches?"

More laughter and hoots. "Give him a facer, Lem!" somebody shouted.

"Believe I'll do just that," Lem answered, doubling up a fist the size of a Virginia ham. "Nobody misses a slice off a cut loaf, huh? One more punch won't matter none."

"Burro," Jenny said quietly, "you better—"

"Never mind," Fargo cut in. "I'll handle this one. Burro, Norton, just keep your eyes on Lupe and Butch—they might try to kill Jenny."

Fargo's real concern was for himself and Buckshot, but he knew the bodyguards didn't give a tinker's damn about either of them. The thug named Lem cocked back his arm and took a step closer to Fargo.

That was the move Fargo had been counting on. His muscle-corded right leg shot up as fast as an arrow leaving the bow. There was a solid thud of impact when the toe of his boot landed exactly on bead, smashing Lem's family jewels.

Lem's face drained of color as if he'd been leeched. He dropped to his knees, making sucking-drain noises, and clutched his crotch. But Fargo wasn't about to let it go at that.

A homicidal rage had been seething beneath the surface since that earlier beating while his hands were tied. Besides, he had two crucial goals to accomplish: convincing these filthy jackals that the legend of Skye Fargo was in fact a real man to be feared; and convincing Jenny Lavoy that she should hitch her star to his wagon, not Butch McDade's.

Fargo took two quick steps backward then shot forward, leaping off the floor and aiming a savage kick at Lem's by now purple face. Fargo kicked *through*, not at, sending yellow stumps of broken teeth spraying like buckshot. He had the satisfaction of hearing the pig-man's neck snap loudly as his head rocketed up and back, shattering the neck vertebrae.

The Bucket of Blood went as silent as a courtroom just before a verdict. The bullyboy flopped onto his back, twitched a few times like a gut-hooked fish, and gave up the ghost in a ghastly death rattle like pebbles caught in a sluice gate.

"What a sockdologer!" somebody said. "Why, Lem's dead as a dried herring!"

"This bearded buckaroo is savage as a meat ax!" another man chimed in, his tone admiring.

There was no real camaraderie in this bunch, only a respect for raw power. Every man in the place stared at Fargo—even El Burro and Norton—visibly impressed. The closest man quickly hopped back out of range of Fargo's lethal legs.

Fargo met Jenny's bewitching brown eyes. Her nostrils flared, her breathing quickening as if she were sexually aroused.

"Well," she said. "Well, well, *well*."

11

The five of them picked their way back to Jenny's house through the gumbo of mud, Jenny silent and contemplative. As they neared the western end of the gulch, she finally spoke up.

"That little demonstration in the saloon, Mr. Fargo, was impressive. But after all, there's never been any doubt that you can be a ruthless killer. The pertinent question is—can you also be a cold-blooded murderer if conditions warrant?"

Again Fargo suspected he was being tested, and bending to her demands too quickly could spell doom for him and Buckshot.

"You act like murder can't be avoided," he replied. "I don't see the need of it. Why cut off your arm at the elbow just to cure a hangnail?"

She whirled toward him. "Oh, why don't you just say it, Pastor Fargo? 'Money is the siren's song that saps our wills!'"

His swollen lips twitched into a lopsided grin. "I doubt if a cyclone could sap your will."

"Murder is just a means to an end. I just rub you the wrong way, don't I? It's all right for a man to figure percentages and angles, to murder, even, but not a woman."

"I don't mind the percentages and angles—nor the curves," he added, his startling blue eyes raking over her. "I just don't like low-down crimes like kidnapping and murder. 'Means to an end'—get off your high horse, lady. You're trying to turn shit into strawberries."

Fargo had deliberately pushed her. The glint in her angry eyes was hard-edged and lethal. "You will remove that reproach or Burro shall remove your organs."

"I apologize," Fargo said. "All I'm saying is that there's smarter and safer ways to get rich."

For the moment, at least, she seemed mollified. "For the record, I have never personally ordered a murder—of any person worthy of life, that is. What my minions do is often beyond my control. I told you it's difficult to find good help."

Fargo and Buckshot avoided looking at each other this time, but both were thinking the same thing: that infant slowly dying in the gulch was in her direct control. And when all the prisoners were murdered, that would be her decision, too.

They returned to the house and Fargo's and Buckshot's hands were untied. They were allowed to wash the blood from their faces at the kitchen pump before they were again banished under guard to "Jenny's jail" as Buckshot had taken to calling it.

"You been playing this deal smart, Fargo," Buckshot said. "That pretty she-devil figures you're circling the bait and close to taking the hook."

Fargo was not as sanguine. "I'm not so sure, old son. She suspects we're sailing under false colors. Even worse, I'm thinking that woman ain't just criminal—she might be out-right insane. She's got the gold fever even worse than some of those forty-niners I saw in the Sierra."

Buckshot rubbed his chin. "Yeah, mebbe you struck a lode there. Did you see that look in her eyes when you done for that cockroach in the saloon—most women woulda been all-overish uncomfortable seeing a sight like that. Mister, *that* gal took to it like all possessed. Might be she's crazy as a loon."

Fargo nodded. "Sometimes crazy people are smart as a steel trap. I found that out when I locked horns with Terrible Jack Slade in Virginia City on the Comstock. Buckshot, this little lass is trouble and nothing but. I'm doing my damnedest to make her think me and you might do to take along, but she's a pretty powder keg that could go up on us at any second."

Toward the middle of the afternoon Norton herded the two men into the kitchen for a tasty meal of bacon, fried potatoes, and Boston brown bread. When Jasmine reached for Fargo's coffee cup to refill it, she dropped a small piece of folded paper under the edge of his plate. It was a bold move, under the watchful eyes of El Burro and Norton, but Fargo managed to palm it without being seen.

Back in the room, keeping a careful eye on the arched doorway, Fargo unfolded it and read it to Buckshot in a whisper, "Guns under Jenny's bed, last room on right as you face gulch."

Fargo popped the note into his mouth and chewed and swallowed it. "That's good to know," he said after he forced the nasty lump down. "But we can't get to the damn things without being shot to rag tatters."

Fargo fell silent for a long time, his mind turning their present fix over and over to study all of its facets.

"I might have an idea," he finally told Buckshot. "It's thin, but it's all I can think of. We really do need to tend to our horses, right?"

"If we still *got* horses."

Fargo explained the plan to Buckshot, who looked dubious but nodded slowly when Fargo had finished.

"Mebbe it could work," he said. "But if it don't, me and you might end up singing the high notes, if you take my drift?"

"I take it, old campaigner. But if it does work, we might kill two birds with one stone. I druther roll the dice on a slim chance than sit around on my duff waiting for her to decide if I live or die."

Fargo made sure his hat was in his hand when he entered the parlor, flanked by the ever-vigilant El Burro and Norton. Jenny sat on the red plush sofa, leafing through a book with colorful illustrations.

"Jasmine tells me you wish to speak with me," Jenny greeted him, adding an enigmatic smile. "Please have a seat, Mr. Fargo."

Fargo dropped into a comfortable chair and balanced his hat on one thigh. "Yes, ma'am. It's about our horses—Buckshot's and mine, I mean."

"Yes, I wondered about that. Over the years I've read various things about this remarkable . . . black stallion, is it?"

"Actually, a black-and-white Ovaro stallion."

"I realize that newspaper writers have a penchant for

'coloring up' the facts, but they make him sound like a winged Pegasus. I understand you're quite fond of him."

"I'm not sure what a winged Pegasus is," Fargo admitted. "As for fond—well, he's just a horse, after all. But a damn good horse. The fastest I've ever seen, and the endurance of a doorknob. There's no end to his bottom."

"Endurance, is it?" She sent him a sly smile. "According to Jasmine, that description fits you. At any rate, where is this horse?"

"Well, you can probably understand why I didn't leave him too near the gulch. He's hidden about a mile away along with Buckshot's grulla—that's a smoky bluish-gray horse and a stallion like mine. We left what water we could but horses are big drinkers. And we brought grain with us, but horses won't eat grain off the ground—by now they've prob'ly cropped off most of the grass they can reach."

"I see. And, of course, you can't bring them into Hangtown, so obviously you want my permission to go feed and water them."

Fargo nodded. "I know it might sound like I'm trying to pull a fast one, but those horses are on loose tethers, and being stallions and all, they just might light out."

She studied him for a full minute, her Mona Lisa smile making his scalp sweat. This serenity was more unnerving—he preferred it when she was all horns and rattles.

"Your request makes sense," she finally said. "And you must realize that only one of you can go. If that one decides to flee, the other will be killed."

Fargo nodded. "I assume that."

"As well you should. I don't really fear an escape under those terms. Whatever moral ambiguities either of you harbor, leaving a good friend to die is not an option, is it?"

Fargo shook his head. "If you have two pails, that's enough water to hold them for a while longer. And I can grain them from my hat and move them to a new patch of graze."

"Yes, but you're leaving something out, aren't you? Something important."

Fargo had anticipated this and he answered forthrightly, "You mean my rifle."

"Yes, this famous repeating rifle that one 'loads on Sunday and fires all year.'"

"All week," he corrected her from a grin.

"Never mind. The main point is that I want you to bring it back with you, Mr. Fargo."

He nodded.

"You'll knock when you return and wait outside for Jasmine's instructions about how to surrender that weapon, is that also clear?"

"Very clear."

Those bewitching brown eyes narrowed to slits. "Now . . . what else are you failing to mention?"

Damn the luck, Fargo thought. He was hoping that acquiring Buckshot's double-ten would throw her off. But obviously she had obtained a very detailed account of the shootout three days ago. This woman talked like a book and didn't miss a trick.

"You must mean Buckshot's rifle?"

"Indeed I do, and coyness is not becoming in a man, Mr. Fargo. I'm disappointed in you. I hoped we were starting to have a meeting of the minds."

El Burro's hand slid toward his curved machete. Clearly he didn't like it when Jenny was disappointed. Fargo felt his back break out in cool sweat.

"All due respect, Miss Lavoy, but the fact that I didn't mention that rifle doesn't mean I had any plans for it."

She studied him for another thirty seconds in silence. "No, it doesn't," she finally conceded. "But you *should* have mentioned it. I assume you'd like to go sometime after sunset?"

He nodded. "I should only need a couple of hours if even that."

"Well, if we do eventually reach a meeting of the minds, obviously I would want you and Mr. Brady to have excellent horses. I like this idea of seizing mining company payrolls. On the other hand, I've come to realize you are a formidable intellect and a worthy foe. It makes perfect sense that you are worried about your horses. But I also fear you are fundamentally decent, and thus, beyond my ability to corrupt and control you."

"A woman as beautiful as you," Fargo said, "shouldn't underrate her ability where men are concerned."

The sincere compliment was a gamble, but it seemed to transform her manner.

"This book I'm perusing," she told him, "is called the *Kama Sutra*. It's a Sanskrit guide to erotic pleasures. Have you ever heard of it?"

He shook his head. She patted the empty cushion beside her. "Come. This section is called 'Positions of Ecstasy.' I'd like to show it to you."

Fargo sat down beside her, drinking in the exotic smell of her perfume. She flipped slowly through the graphically illustrated pages, carefully watching his face.

"Well?" she demanded after showing him several pages.

Fargo shrugged. "Nice pictures, but I didn't learn anything new, if that's what you mean."

"You mean, none of this shocks or offends you?"

"Nah. It's pretty old hat."

"You don't mean to say you've actually . . . employed all of these positions?"

Fargo grinned. "I'd say enjoyed, not employed."

"Even *this* one?" She pointed to one where the man and woman looked like two snakes swallowing each other.

Fargo nodded. "Yeah. It put a kink in my neck, though."

"I never would have thought . . ." Her voice trailed off on a note of wonder. "Well, perhaps you *will* do."

"What for, may I ask?"

"There's one page I'm not showing you yet. It's not so much a position as a . . . well, a rare technique and a longtime fantasy of mine. I'm afraid, however, that you might balk—I assure you, it's new even to *your* apparently vast experience."

"Don't count me out just yet," Fargo said. "With me it's always the woman's choice."

"We'll see about that. Talk is cheap. As for your request about your horses—I've decided to let you go. But first, *look* at me."

Fargo did, staring into that classically beautiful face whose eyes probed him to his core. Those intrusive, knowing eyes searched deep into his, seeking the secret bastion of his very soul.

"You're up to something," she finally decided. "You're very clever and a good dissembler, but I can see it. You've met your match in me, Skye Fargo. 'All hope abandon, ye who enter here.' Hope, Mr. Fargo, will get you and your friend killed."

An hour after sundown Fargo set out. Under Burro's watchful eye Buckshot was permitted outside long enough to hand the pails up to Fargo at the lip of the shallow gulch. The thick ring of protective brush forced him to work the pails through one at a time.

The vast indigo velvet sky was peppered silver with stars, and a cool, steady breeze made Fargo grateful to be free again, albeit only temporarily. He was suffering from cooped-up fever in the small, windowless room and longed to be spreading his blankets again to the backdrop of humming cicadas and the sweet serenade of the western wind.

Jenny Lavoy was absolutely right, he told himself as he carefully hauled the pails across the open, rock-strewn terrain—he was on the wrong side of the "power balance" and he didn't like it one damn bit. The plan he had in mind was reckless and fraught with difficulties. But desperate situations called for desperate remedies. So far he and Buckshot were simply barking at a knot—sometimes even the wrong action was better than no action at all.

All hope abandon, ye who enter here. Jenny Lavoy's smug tone, as she spoke those words, now brought a flush of anger to Fargo's face. She was telling him to either submit to the rudder or crash on the rocks.

"Screw you, bitch," he muttered into the wind. "I'll take the rocks any day."

As he approached the grassy draw where they'd tethered their horses, apprehension filled him like a bucket under a tap. If those two high-spirited stallions had literally pulled up stakes and lit out for parts unknown, he and Buckshot were even more hopelessly trapped in a world of hurt. Their only option then would be outlaw horses, assuming they could acquire any.

A welcoming whicker from the Ovaro, who had caught his scent on the wind, tugged Fargo's lips into a smile.

He topped the low ridge above the draw and spotted both horses in the silver-white moonlight.

"You two are a sight for sore eyes," he greeted them.

Fargo let each horse drink half a pail of water and poured the rest into the little oilskin-lined cistern. He opened the bag of crushed barley lying beside his saddle and held it up so each horse got a good feed. Then he pulled their pickets and moved them into lush grass where they could still reach the water.

Fargo spent a few minutes scratching each mount on the withers and talking to them gently to calm their nervousness.

"Stick it out a bit longer, old campaigner," he told his Ovaro. "I know you want to run and stretch out the kinks."

Fargo slid the Henry and the North & Savage from their boots, rigging the slings and hanging them around both his shoulders. He would surrender them, all right—Buckshot's life was forfeit if he didn't.

But there was one remaining weapon Jenny "Little Britches" Lavoy could not know about, and it was probably his and Buckshot's last, desperate chance.

Fargo unbuckled a saddle pocket and pulled out the French Lefaucheux six-shot pinfire revolver. The ornately detailed weapon was beautiful and included a foldaway knife blade under the barrel. Fargo had accepted it, during a riverboat poker game in New Orleans, in lieu of a cash bet.

Unfortunately, pinfire cartridges were hard to come by nowadays and there were only two in the wheel. Even worse, they were made of paper and hadn't been replaced in years. There was a good chance the powder had clumped by now and wouldn't ignite, nor could Fargo afford to waste one testing them.

At least the knife blade was sturdy and well mounted, he noted, examining it in the moonlight. Compared to the huge blade of his confiscated Arkansas toothpick, it was poor shakes as a fighting knife. Against formidable men like El Burro and Norton—especially El Burro—he would have to make the very first thrust count for score.

But the biggest risk of all, Fargo realized, would be hiding and then retrieving the pinfire revolver. He would certainly never get through the door with it tonight.

"Pile on the agony," he muttered as he tucked the revolver into his belt and set out toward the gulch.

At the lip of the gulch he stretched out and let each rifle slide down to the bottom, followed by the pails. Then he scrabbled down and looked carefully around to see if one of the guards was lurking to spy on him. Spotting no one, he left everything else where it was and hurried around to the back of the rickety wooden privy.

Waiting for wind gusts to cover the noise, Fargo grabbed the end of one of the weathered gray planks and tugged it until the sharpened wooden peg, used instead of nails, gave way. He pushed the board back flush with the rest of them and laid the pinfire on the ground. If one of the guards found it before he retrieved it, Jenny Lavoy's wrath might prove deadly—to him.

He gathered up everything, carried it to the house, and thonked on the door with the side of his fist.

"Skye, is that you?" Jasmine's voice called out.

"Right down to the ground. Give me my instructions."

"Just leave the pails outside. Miss Lavoy told me to tell you that I'm in the line of fire between you and El Burro."

"I understand, hon. No parlor tricks."

"I'll crack the door open a few inches. You stick each rifle inside one at a time, stock first, so I can grab it."

A wedge of light winked into view when the door meowed open. Fargo handed in first the Henry, then the North & Savage.

"All right," she said. "Now put both your empty hands inside the door first, then leave them in view and come on in."

As soon as Fargo was inside, Jasmine moved aside while Burro, jabbing the muzzle of one of his Colt Navy revolvers into Fargo's gut, searched him thoroughly—so thoroughly that Fargo remarked, "Ease off—that ain't a gun barrel you're pinching, old son. Or have you forgotten?"

El Burro backhanded him so hard that Fargo bounced off the hallway wall. He tended to rile cool, a trait that increased longevity on the frontier. But Fargo made a mark in his ledger of accounts.

El Burro nodded to Jasmine, who called out, "All secure, Miss Lavoy!"

Jenny stepped through the nearest curtained archway. "Well, Mr. Fargo, are your horses still where you left them?"

"Yes, and now fed and watered. Thanks for letting me go, Miss Lavoy."

"I hope you didn't abuse my trust?"

"That would be a fool's errand given the circumstances."

"And you're no fool, right?"

"Not tonight anyway."

She gave him her tinkling, silver-smooth laugh. Then, abruptly, the stunning face hardened. "I suspect you're lying, Mr. Fargo. Once again our minds are pitted one against the other. It's a contest I rather enjoy."

"Tell you the truth, I could do without it."

"I'm sure. And may God have mercy on your soul if you lose."

12

"How'd it go?" Buckshot whispered as Fargo pulled off his boots.

"The horses are all right. And the pinfire's behind the crapper with a board in front of it loosened up. But Her Nibs is watching damn close for a fox play."

Fargo stretched out on his pallet, realizing how bone-tired he was. His face still ached from that morning's beating, and carrying two full pails of water for over a mile had left his shoulders feeling like they'd been hammered. He recalled the goading grin on El Burro's face, the stun of his hard-hitting fists, and the anger seethed within him again.

"We best make our play damn fast," Buckshot said. "That she-bitch has twigged our game, Skye."

Something ominous in Buckshot's tone made Fargo alert like a hound on point. "What's your drift?"

"Plenty happened while you was gone. First she had Norton take me into the parlor so's she could question me. She said she knew you was up to something, and she wanted to know what it was. She nagged me half haywire about it."

"Yeah, so? You weren't stupid enough to tell her?"

"Sell your ass, churn-brain," Buckshot retorted. "But that pert skirt put the hoodoo eye on me. I ain't as smooth a liar as you. I kept telling her you was only worried about our horses. But . . . hell 'n' furies! She's got this way of lookin' right into a man's thoughts."

"She did it to me, too," Fargo admitted. "Damn it, Buckshot, that woman gives me goose pimples. Jangles my nerves. I ain't even sure I got the guts to try this play with the pinfire. I've whipped Comanches, Kiowas, Apaches, won walking showdowns with lead-chuckers like Red Lassiter and Big Bat Landry, tracked down and killed that insane arsonist Blaze Weston. I've survived fire, flood, stampedes, and jealous husbands firing blue whistlers at me. And *still* that little cottontail gives me the jimmy leg."

"You and me both, chappie. She's a mighty potent force. I like to shit my pants when she put that hoodoo eye on me. Anyhow, that ain't all. Butch McDade was here after you lit out."

"You heard them?"

"I heard *that* bullhorn, yeah—leastways, part of what he said. I couldn't make out nothing Jenny said. They musta been hobnobbing about that ransom plan she's got for you. I heard him mention newspapers and somethin' 'bout having a man take her letter to the Pony Express way station at Thunder Butte."

"That's eighty or so miles from here," Fargo said. "If she does send a letter, it'll get to Saint Joe in about five days."

"You think she'll do it? Might be she's just stringing Butch along—'member what she told him, how they'd work the details out later?"

Fargo expelled a sigh of frustration. "Hell, how can you know with her? I don't trust one damn thing she says. Anyhow, it doesn't matter. It would be weeks, at least, before any ransom delivery could show up, and we sure's hell can't let this thing stretch on much longer. You think that sick baby we saw this morning can hang on for weeks?"

"Not even one week. And the rest of them folks don't look too chirpy, neither."

"One thing's certain," Fargo said. "When I brought that pinfire back, I set the clock ticking. We can't fiddle around now. The longer it stays where I put it, the greater the chance of discovery. And one hard rain would soak those paper cartridges. But even if I manage to sneak it into this room, Jenny's suspicious of us now. This room *will* be searched, count on it."

"One of us could pull it inside and toss it down the crapper," Buckshot suggested. "Leastways we'd be shut of it. Or we can draw lots, and one of us can come outta that shithouse a-smokin'. Both of them dickless bastards wait outside for us."

Fargo mulled that. "It'd be dicey, old son. If the powder loads have clumped, sure as cats fighting they'll burn both of us down before you can say Jack Robinson. Still, it might be our best chance, at that. But we won't draw lots—you've never used that gun before."

"It's a goldang mess," Buckshot muttered.

"It is," Fargo said, confidence seeping back into his tone. "But a mess can be cleaned up."

The next morning marked one full week since the raid up north on Ed Creighton's work crew. To Fargo, nerves stretched drumhead tight on tenterhooks, it felt like a lifetime since he had been a free man riding under western skies.

He and Buckshot were awake before Jenny's mute bodyguards came to fetch them.

"I've had my bellyful of that beautiful little bitch, old son," Fargo told Buckshot in a low, grim tone as he yanked on his boots. "This morning we either win the horse or lose the saddle. That pinfire is small caliber, so when I bust out of that crapper I'm going for two head shots, savvy?"

"Naught else for it," Buckshot agreed. "Only a head shot guarantees a one-bullet kill."

"Now listen up. I'll have the foldaway blade in place. If that shooter don't fire, I'm going through El Burro's ribs and into his heart with the blade. If that happens, you'll have to jump Norton. Lock his gun hand up at the wrist long enough for me to get one of the Burro's Colts and kill Norton."

"Lotta 'ifs' and 'ands,'" Buckshot fretted. "But it's come down to the nut-cuttin' now, I reckon. Don't forget the she-bitch. She'll hear the ruckus, and she's heeled with that little hideout gun—not to mention all our weapons."

"Yeah, it's Patsy I'm most worried about. If she turns both those barrels on us, they'll hafta bury us with a rake. So we get inside the house quick—I mean faster than a finger snap."

"Do we kill her, Skye?"

Fargo tugged on his close-cropped beard. "She deserves it, all right, but I've never killed a woman and I'm not eager to do it. She just might force our hand—she's a scrappy little vixen. If we can get to her fast enough, we'll bind and gag her. We've got plenty of work ahead of us if we mean to get out of this gulch alive. Those prisoners have to go with us."

It was a desperate plan, all right, but Fargo had faced long odds all his life. However, ten minutes later, one simple unforeseen act turned all of it into mere mental vapors: El Burro left the door wide open while Fargo and Buckshot took turns in the privy, never once taking his eyes off them.

Fargo had been right in his surmise of the night before: Jenny suspected him and Buckshot of treachery. Making matters worse—while El Burro held them under the gun, Norton scrambled up the back wall of the gulch and beat the bushes. If they thought to search behind the outhouse, Fargo realized, yesterday's beating would seem like a lover's caress compared to what was coming.

"Good morning, gentlemen," Jenny greeted them in the kitchen. "I trust you slept well?"

The constant ironic edge to her tone got on Fargo's nerves. It implied she was one up on the rest of the world and any fools in fringed buckskins.

Jasmine served up plates of pandowdy and bacon while Jenny sipped tea and watched the two men like a cat on a rat.

"Jasmine," she said casually, "please put on more water to boil." Then she looked at Fargo.

"Mr. Fargo," she said, "it's often said that one can't hitch a horse with a coyote. But isn't it true that a horse and a coyote will cooperate for their mutual survival?"

Fargo chewed, swallowed, and looked at her, trying to figure her angle. "Well, I've seen animals that usually attack each other share a small spit of land in a flood, if that's what you mean."

"Yes, I've heard of such things. I'm getting very close to a critical juncture—whether to go with the status quo here in the gulch or trust you two to help me establish a new order, so to speak."

"The hell's a status quo?" Buckshot interjected.

She ignored him, still watching Fargo closely. "I have very little time to make that decision."

"I don't follow you," Fargo said. "Yesterday you had your two lickspittles here"—El Burro scowled darkly—"beat hell out of our faces. You figured it would buy you some time after you paraded us around so the rest could see us."

"That was the general idea, yes, and it would have worked. But I didn't anticipate your rather impressive killing of Lem Aldrich. Yes, it fascinated those baboons in the saloon. By now, however, it has begun to rankle in their craws, as the idiom goes. In the main they are a pack of cowardly curs. But even a toothless dog will bite if kicked hard enough."

"Miss Lavoy," Buckshot spoke up again, "I don't cotton none to being a prisoner here. But I ain't never knowed a woman who can figure out men like you can."

"It requires no great skill," she dismissed him. "Most men think with their cods. Not until a man grows so old he is no longer piss-proud in the morning does he develop any wisdom."

Fargo was astounded yet again. This woman looked every inch the great lady, but her brutal frankness was unnerving.

"But as I was saying," she resumed, her intensely probing eyes pinning Fargo by his soul, "the issue with you two is trust."

"Here's the way of it," Fargo said. "If we just come out and tell you that you can trust us, that we want to throw in with you, you'll just figure we're lying to you in hopes of escaping. So where does that leave us?"

"It leaves us with your *actions*. As the line goes, I can't hear what you say because what you are speaks too loudly. So far you *appear* to have been good little boys. But Jasmine has certainly been a bad little girl."

Jasmine, standing at the cookstove waiting for the tea kettle to boil, paled at these words. "Ma'am?"

"Don't play the ingenue with me, you treacherous little whore. The next time you write a note to Mr. Fargo, make sure you tear the page off the pad first. That way you'll avoid leaving a faint imprint on the next page."

Jasmine flinched as if struck by a bolt out of the blue. Her legs suddenly went so weak she had to clutch the soapstone sink beside her. Fargo felt his blood seem to stop and flow backward as the words from that one-line note he had eaten now sparked in his memory: *Guns under Jenny's bed . . .*

Jenny Lavoy's face was a mask of sadistic purpose. "Is that water boiling?"

"Yes," Jasmine managed in a breathless whisper.

"Fine. Norton, place one gun behind each man's head, full cock. If either one so much as twitches, paper the wall with their brains. Burro, pin the blond whore's arms behind her and bend her over the sink—yes, like that."

Jenny rose to the stove and grasped the kettle. "Jasmine, you have a pretty face although you're a bit bucktoothed. Before I pour this boiling water on it and make you a hideous monster forever, I have one question: did Mr. Fargo ask you to look for those guns, or did you volunteer the information?"

"I . . ." Words failed her, and if Burro hadn't been holding her up, Jasmine would have collapsed to the floor.

"I told her to look for them," Fargo volunteered. "Your dicker is with me, not her."

"Then I will give you a choice: her pretty face or your handsome one?"

Buckshot was chewing on his lip so hard it was bleeding. But by now Fargo was filled with a quiet rage and had no more fear in him than a rifle.

"Tell you what, lady. Before you pour that water on either of us, you're gonna have to kill me."

"Kill *us*," Buckshot amended.

"And once you kill us," Fargo said, "what then? You know damn good and well you're scared spitless of that bunch of filthy hyenas in the gulch. Power is a two-way street; the same ones who give it to you will take it away. And once they do, El Burro and Norton won't be able to stop those filthy, lice-ridden mongrels from mounting you until they rape you to death."

Jenny surprised everyone present by laughing like a gay little school girl who had tricked the class.

"You needn't be so melodramatic, Mr. Fargo. I've grown quite fond of Jasmine and I have no intention of scalding her face. Nor yours. And for your information, your weapons will remain under my bed—I'm not willing yet to place them back in your hands. Norton, lower your guns, please. Jasmine dear, have a seat for a few minutes until you quit shaking."

Jenny removed the kettle from the stove and poured another pot of tea to brew. "Skye," she said, using his front name for the first time, "I'm growing something akin to fond of you, too. But your assessment of my danger is too dire—you underestimate my control over Butch McDade and Lupe Cruz, and overestimate your importance to my survival. The blunt truth is this: either you two are going to die or those three are, depending which decision will make me a richer woman. It's purely business."

She turned those direct-as-searchlight eyes first on Buckshot, then Fargo, as she added, "I'll let the situation with the note go—it's harmless enough since you'll never get at those guns. Besides, Skye, you and I have an erotic tryst coming up soon. But try my patience just once more, and I'll cast my lot with Butch McDade. Lacking your cunning mind, he's easier to control."

Fargo thought about that gun lying behind the outhouse and told himself again, scalp sweating: *She's mad as a March hare.*

"Boys, for a time there I was sittin' on the anxious seat," Butch McDade announced. "But what I seen yesterday sets my mind at ease. Little Britches had Fargo and his pard worked over pretty good. She sure's hell ain't lipping salt from his hand, hey? Don't look to me like she's got any big idea about dealing him in and us out."

He passed a bottle of red-eye across the table to Lupe Cruz. Cruz knocked back a slug and wiped his mouth on his sleeve before passing the bottle to Waldo Tate. Night was settling over Hangtown and the three men could hear a raucous din from the nearby Bucket of Blood.

"I saw something yesterday," Cruz said, "that did *not* set my mind at ease. *Maldita!* Even with his *manos* tied behind him, this Fargo killed a man. Butch, even if he has not—how you say—beguiled Jenny, Fargo is a dangerous man."

"You ain't birding there," Butch agreed. "Give Fargo just *that* much chance"—he snapped his fingers—"and he'll sink us six feet closer to hell. All I'm saying is that Jenny wouldn't have her geldings play thump-thump with him if her and him was chummy."

111

Waldo shook his head. "I got the fantods, Butch. I still think Jenny means to buck us three out, and it's Fargo she'll use to do it."

"You best do a pecker check," Butch scoffed, "and make sure you're a man."

"I'm telling you," Waldo insisted, "Jenny's caught a spark for that bastard, and now us three will get the hind tit—or worse."

McDade's insolent lips twisted in scorn. "What, a little bird told you all this? Or maybe you got one of them crystal balls?"

"No, I heard it with my own ears."

McDade had started to raise the bottle to his lips. Now he set it down, staring at Waldo. "Spell that out."

"I was in the Temple yesterday when she came in with Fargo and the 'breed. And I'm telling you those two were palsy-walsy. She thought I was too stoned to make sense of anything, but I heard everything she said to him."

"Like what, f'rinstance?"

"Stuff you wouldn't be saying to some jasper who was just a prisoner you wanted to ransom. She told him how she allowed the Temple because the drugs control us men—'a brake on men's wilder impulses' she called it. She asked Fargo if he ever used the pipe, and when he said no, she looked satisfied as all hell—said that was good because a man had to be ready at all times or some shit. Now you tell me: *why* would she be talking that way to a man she planned to ransom off and kill? You ask me, they were talking like they were closing a deal."

"Hell, Waldo, you was smoking tar balls. That stuff addles a man's brains."

"Tar balls ain't like peyote," Waldo insisted. "It makes me feel like I'm floating, sort of, and gives me strange dreams. But it actually makes my hearing sharper. I heard every damn word. And, Butch, I'm telling you straight from the shoulder—they were talking chummy."

"Hell, you boys know how strange Jenny is. Look how she was right before she had the Burro kill Boots Winkler—why, her tone was dripping honey."

"This is true," Lupe put in, his face troubled. "But a thing

112

troubles me—*why* did she march Fargo and his friend all over the gulch so all of us could see they had been beaten? As you just said, Butch, it set your mind at ease. Was that perhaps her plan all along? To—how you say—to . . ."

"Allay our suspicions," Waldo supplied.

Lupe nodded. "*Eso es.* The very thing."

McDade's habitual sneer twisted into a frown. "That is a mite queer, ain't it? And Fargo killing Lem like he done— that look on Jenny's face, almost like she was telling the men there was a new sheriff in town."

"Now you're snapping wise," Waldo approved. "Boys, the smartest thing we can do is saddle up and light a shuck out of this gulch. Jenny figures there's too many pigs for the tits, and *we* are the three little pigs she means to have Fargo slaughter first."

Butch slammed a fist into the table. "Damn it all, Waldo, even if that's all true, why get snow in your boots? We got a good setup here, and Lupe was right—Jenny ain't the problem; it's Fargo. You're the one with the good think-piece on his shoulders. Scratch us up a plan."

"I already have," Waldo replied. "I knew you wouldn't agree to light out, so I have an idea that's even better than just killing Fargo and his sidekick—it takes out the Burro and Norton, too, and leaves Jenny helpless without us. It also pulls in the rest of the men."

"Well, do I have to beat it out of you?"

"You know how damn bored the men are, and how much they like to wager. So we announce a knife fight between Lupe and Fargo and we take the bets. We act like Jenny's already agreed to it and get the men all het up on the idea, see?"

Waldo glanced at Lupe. "I'm assuming you got no objections?"

Lupe's teeth flashed out of his dusky face. He caressed the cord-wrapped hilt of his dag by way of reply. Then something occurred to him.

"*Por dios!* You have seen what Fargo can do with his legs."

"Yeah, I thought about that. So we announce the fight is going to be a Mexican standoff."

"The hell's that?" Butch demanded.

Lupe grinned. "The two—how you say—opponents' left

113

wrists are tied together. The fight begins with their knives held straight overhead in their right hands. I have killed several men in standoffs like this. Best of all, we will be too close for Fargo to mount a good kick."

"Right," Waldo said, "but we have to let on that the fight is *not* to the death, or Jenny will never go along with it—remember her claim that Fargo is a 'valuable asset.'"

"So she says," Butch interjected. "She's still sandbagging on writing the ransom letter."

"Anyway," Waldo concluded, "we make out that whoever draws first blood is the winner, no killing allowed."

"Yeah, but Jenny still might not play along," Butch objected. "You know how she raises holy hell when we cook up something without getting her say-so."

"That's the genius of my plan," Waldo boasted. "She won't know we cooked it up. We get the men fired up on it, then go to her and claim they're the ones demanding it. You know how she tries to keep them happy. We'll tell her they might riot if they don't get some good entertainment. She'll fall in line."

Butch pondered all of this and finally nodded. "Sure, and Lupe cuts the son of a bitch open from neck to nuts. But, say—Fargo gets around, he likely knows Lupe's reputation as a knife fighter. How do we know he'll string along?"

"Do not worry about Fargo," Lupe said. "He and his Arkansas toothpick are also *famoso*. He is a confident man."

"And a strutting peacock," Waldo added. "He won't back down in front of Jenny."

"All right, but I don't see how the Burro and Norton figure in," Butch said. "Them two got eyes in the back of their heads."

"They're mighty vigilant," Waldo agreed. "But no man—not even a gelded one—can resist a good knife fight. They'll be the most distracted at the moment Lupe guts Fargo. That's when we open up on them. Sure, Jenny will throw a hissy fit, but tough tit. What can she do about it? The rest of the men don't like them two freaks, either. We'll be all she has left to control the others and she knows it."

Butch leveled an admiring gaze on Waldo. "Tate, I knew I kept a soft-handed pus-gut like you around for some reason.

It's a good plan. But both you boys remember one thing: we can't set this deal up until day after tomorrow at the earliest. We got no idea what Jenny and Fargo might spring on us before then. That lanky bastard is six sorts of trouble, and that 'breed siding him looks mighty consequential, too. Either we all pull together or we all cop it."

13

As Fargo had feared, there was no chance to grab that pinfire on the third morning of his and Buckshot's captivity—again the door to the privy was left open when the prisoners relieved themselves. El Burro and Norton watched both men, short guns leveled on them, as silent and vigilant as the Swiss Guard protecting the Pope.

Jenny Lavoy, usually talkative at breakfast, was oddly silent as the two men tied into stacks of buckwheat cakes smothered in molasses. She merely sipped her tea and watched Fargo from speculative eyes that made his armpits break out in sweat.

"That little slyboots is up to something," he told Buckshot after the two men were herded back to the room that had become their prison cell.

"Ain't she always? Mebbe she's come to her decision 'bout whether to stick with McDade's bunch or throw in with us. Way she talked yestiddy, she made it clear she had to shit or get off the pot, and quick."

"Yeah, and don't forget what else she said—whoever she sided with, the other side had to die."

"Uh-huh. She also said you and her had a whatchacallit first . . ."

"An 'erotic tryst.'"

"Don't that mean screwin'?"

"It would with a normal woman. With her, you pay your money and take your chances."

"Mebbe," Buckshot suggested, "she's like them female spiders that kill the male after they mate."

Fargo sent him a baleful glance. "Why'n't you just caulk up?"

"That shit she done yestiddy to Jasmine makes me ireful," Buckshot remarked. "Didja see how pale and scairt that poor gal was this morning? She's a plumb good sort."

"Yeah. At first I figured she was lucky not to be stuck with the rest of the prisoners. Now I'm not so sure."

Buckshot cursed hotly. "It's the same old story. After you play slap 'n' tickle with Her Nibs, you can brag how you poked the two prettiest gals in this God-forgotten gulch. And what's old Buckshot get—jack, that's what."

"Right now, old son, I'd be grateful for a real saloon with sawdust on the floor and sporting girls topside."

"I druther have the sawdust topside and the sporting gals on the floor with me riding them like a bronc buster. Damn it, Fargo, I got cabin fever. This shit with us just waitin' around to be murdered ain't our nach'ral gait."

"There's always a hole card, Buckshot. We just have to turn it up in time and hope it's a trump."

"Hole card, my hairy white ass! What you mean is we best pull a rabbit out of a hat, and mighty damn quick."

Buckshot leaned closer to Fargo and whispered in his ear. "It's only Norton sittin' out in the hall. Should we just bust through the curtains and jump him?"

Fargo, fearing that their demise might be only a fox step away, had been pondering the same move himself. But Norton, like Burro, was fanatical in his devotion to, and protection of, Jenny. His chair was about ten feet back from the archway, his reflexes sharp as a cat's—and Fargo had always respected the truism that a bullet was faster than any man.

"It's damn near a hopeless move," he whispered back, "but I'd do it in two shakes if I believed in my gut Jenny means to order us killed. But I don't—I think there's an even chance she'll decide to deal us in. And an even chance beats a hopeless move."

Buckshot immediately saw the truth of that and nodded. "That shines, Trailsman. But damn her pretty bones to hell, she best decide quick. We got to make our big play soon. Even if she lets us keep feeding and watering our horses, you know damn good and well they can't survive long withouten they bust loose."

Fargo knew exactly what he meant. Even in a protected

draw, those horses were a magnet for danger. Roving Indians could find them, or they could draw the attention of wolf packs or pumas. They'd already been there too long.

Fargo was about to reply when El Burro appeared in the doorway, almost blocking it out. Jenny peeked around him, her enigmatic smile back.

"Come, Mr. Fargo," she said.

A ball of ice replaced Fargo's stomach, but he held his face impassive as he rose to his feet. Buckshot met his glance briefly and both men wondered the same thing: was this the end of the trail at last? Fargo accepted the fact of death as did any Western drifter, for on the frontier death was always as real as a man riding beside you. But to die like a hog led to slaughter—that Fargo could not accept.

"Come where, Miss Lavoy?"

Two menacing clicks as the Burro thumbed his hammers to full cock.

"How foolish of me to ask," Fargo said drily as he headed out of the room.

He was led down the hallway toward the front of the house. At the last archway on the right, Jenny's room, she pulled the curtains aside. "How do you like it?"

Again Fargo was struck at how she had transformed this old fur traders' winter quarters into a luxurious habitation with stolen merchandise. He took in a bed with a ruffled canopy and satin pillows, a triple-mirror vanity, thick Persian rugs.

But it was the strange object dangling from the center crossbeam that she was talking about: a giant wicker basket suspended from an ingenious system of ropes, blocks, and pulleys.

"El Burro made it," she said proudly. "Isn't he clever?"

"I don't know," Fargo replied. "The hell is it?"

"It's called the basket of ecstasy in English," she explained, her voice tightening an octave with excitement as she gazed at it. "It's from that erotic manual I showed you—the *Kama Sutra*. For years I've been wanting to try it."

Fargo speared his fingers through his hair, perplexed. "Looks to me like you've got a fine bed. It won't be easy for two people to squeeze into that basket. Nor very comfortable."

She laughed and made a deprecatory motion with her

hand. "Fat lot *you* know. Never mind, you'll learn all about it when I send for you this evening. Are you looking forward to our tryst?"

Fargo's eyes swept over her from the intricately braided brown hair and Greek goddess face to the petite, tautly curved body highlighted to perfection in a pinch-waisted lavender dress. The low-cut bodice showed a generous portion of her creamy breasts, thrust high by tight stays.

"Is Paris a city?" he replied. His eyes shifted back to the basket. "But that contraption . . . I don't get it."

"Oh, we're *both* going to get it," she promised him. "Like you've never had it before. I assure you, Mr. Fargo, that even a man of your vast carnal experience is going to be astounded by a sensual experience you've never even imagined."

By now her pitch had hooked him. But when Fargo glanced at the Burro, whose cocked revolvers were two deadly, unblinking eyes staring him down, he couldn't help recalling Buckshot's remark:

Mebbe she's like them female spiders that kill the male after they mate.

The morning dragged by like a parade of snails, the two prisoners playing no-pot poker, pacing like caged animals, and reminiscing about adventures that now seemed a lifetime behind them.

Just past noon they heard loud knocking on the front door. Fargo moved to the curtains and cocked his head, listening. It didn't take long to detect the gravelly, blustery voice of Butch McDade. At first Jenny's voice was just a musical murmur, but as the discussion apparently heated up, her voice grew more strident.

Fargo could make out very little, especially whatever Jenny said. But snatches of McDade's talk reached him occasionally like distant sounds wafting on the wind:

". . . not my idea, damn it . . . what the men want . . . bets already . . . and if Fargo . . . nobody killed . . ."

Jenny's voice rose one final time, the door slammed, and a cloak of ominous silence fell over the house.

"What's the grift?" Buckshot demanded. "Jenny sounded all exfluctuated."

Fargo lifted a shoulder. "Damned if I know. But Her Nibs definitely doesn't like it. I heard my name, too."

"Hunh. Mebbe he's after her to write that ransom letter."

"Could be, I s'pose. Somehow I don't think so. Judging by her tone, there's something new on the spit and she doesn't like it."

"And I'll bet a dollar to a doughnut we ain't gonna like it none, neither. That Butch McDade is bad cess. And us without any shooters."

"We've got one," Fargo reminded him in a sarcastic tone. "But it might's well be under her bed with the rest for all the good it does us."

"Speaking 'bout her bed, Trailsman, sounds like you're gonna be in it soon. See if you can't dangle one hand down and fill it with blue steel while you're trimming her."

"Yeah," Fargo said absently. He had said nothing to Buckshot about that basket dangling from her ceiling—he couldn't puzzle it out himself much less explain it to anyone else.

"God's trousers," Buckshot added. "They say two's company and three's a riot. You don't think she'll have one of them dickless wonders in the room with you two, hanh?"

Fargo stopped pacing. "I never thought of that. I don't mind women watching, but I draw the line at a man—even a gelding."

"You done it with gals watching?"

"Sure, when I'm doing two at once."

Buckshot cursed. "Fargo, you greedy son of a bitch." But after a pause curiosity got the best of him. "*How* can you do two at one time? A man ain't got but one pizzle."

"Never mind that, you old whoremonger. We got bigger fish to fry."

The day dragged on some more, broken up only by a quick march to the kitchen for a plate of soda biscuits smothered in flour gravy. When Fargo judged it was nearly sunset, El Burro and Jenny again showed up in the doorway.

She crooked her finger in a beckoning motion. "Come along, Mr. Fargo."

Mr. Fargo . . . The Trailsman just couldn't fathom this woman. She was about to drop her linen for him, yet still stood on formalities. Was she going to make him sign a contract, too?

"El Burro will be right outside in the hallway," she informed Fargo, "and Norton has instructions to kill your friend at the first sign of trouble. So be on your best behavior."

"You do know how to put a man in the mood," he jibed.

"Don't play the wounded cavalier, Mr. Fargo. Are 'moods' really necessary for a stallion like you to perform?"

"No," he admitted, hoisted on his own petard.

"And like you, I have no need for proper moods. I don't hug. I don't kiss. I don't submit to caresses. In fact, I don't even like to touch a man when I use him for my pleasure—except, of course, the one part I need. Thus, we're going to try this."

By now they were in her room. She pointed at the pulley-and-block rigged basket suspended from the crossbeam.

"The only reason I'm stripping," she informed him in a no-nonsense tone, "is to get you aroused. Do *not* touch me."

Fargo had bagged some strange quail in his time, including a gal in the Rockies who insisted they do it in the saddle while the Ovaro galloped. But this one took the blue ribbon for queer notions. However, all that was flushed from his mind after she'd peeled off her clothing. She was almost a foot shorter than he, a creamy little erotic doll with plum-tipped tits that rode high and came directly at him like artillery shells.

"Drop your trousers," she ordered like an army doctor inspecting recruits for hernias.

He unbuckled his belt and let his buckskins slide down. When she saw his curved saber, blood-swollen and bobbing, her eyes widened in disbelief.

"Jasmine didn't exaggerate one bit," she said, her tone fretful. "Damn it, it might be too big for the hole."

"It's never been too big for any woman," Fargo assured her.

"Not *my* hole, you handsome stallion. *This* hole."

She pointed into the wicker basket. Fargo did a double take. A hole had been cut in the very center of the bottom, the edges well padded with silk.

"What the hell . . . ?"

She grabbed the *Kama Sutra* manual off the bed. "Here's

one of the pages I didn't show you," she explained, thrusting it before his startled face. "See how it works? The woman is in full control—the man just lays there and enjoys it."

Fargo studied the vivid illustration. The skeptical look slowly ebbed from his face.

"Well, now," he finally said. "With me it's always the woman's choice."

"I doubt if you could pronounce the Sanskrit name for it," she added. "Just think of it as snatch-in-a-basket."

She climbed in and squatted down. "When I pull this rope on the right, the basket goes up; the rope on the left drops it down. There's a folded-up quilt under it—when I raise the basket up high enough, you lie under it and line your pecker up with the hole. If it fits all right, I'll do the rest."

She was a few bricks short of a load, all right, but Fargo found it an exciting kind of crazy. Jenny easily raised the basket and Fargo stretched out under it, carefully scootching to just the right spot.

"Fits just fine," he reported.

The basket jiggled a little as she positioned herself perfectly over the opening. She tugged the left rope and a wondrous, tight, hot velvet glove wrapped his blue-veiner.

Both of them gasped with pleasure at the same time. Jenny began tugging left-right, left-right in an expert rhythm that increased in tempo as her breathing grew ragged and loud. Up to the very tip, down again in gliding ecstasy, over and over, sending galvanic pleasure surges exploding through him.

He saw her face appear briefly over the edge of the basket, blushing red with excited blood. "You're *huge*," she praised. "It feels like you're up to my navel! Now reach up and twirl the basket!"

Fargo followed orders, and suddenly he felt that new "sensuous sensation" she had promised earlier in the day. Up-down, up-down, spinning first clockwise and then counterclockwise as the rope untwisted itself. As if that wasn't enough pleasure, she pumped and squeezed with her love muscle, a pleasure overload.

A few minutes of this and Fargo felt the floodgates about to burst open. As his staff swelled and tightened for imminent release, she cried out, "Oh no, you don't!"

Even swept up in delirious pleasure, Fargo felt a sharp jolt of fear when she stopped tugging the ropes long enough to flash her over-and-under gun at him. "If you *dare* finish before I do," she panted hoarsely, "I'll shoot you!"

"Christ sakes, lady," he panted back, "get your finger off that trigger! I'll do my best."

Right-left, right-left, up and down, faster, even faster, Jenny beginning to whimper like a bitch in heat as Fargo made a Herculean effort to hold off. Finally she went for the strong finish and cried out, "Now, Fargo! GET IT!"

Strong spasms jerked him like a fish in the bottom of a boat as he spent himself. Jenny gave out a strange warbling sound, the basket wobbling and jerking as she, too, lost all control. Slowly it settled again into a dead hang as, for uncounted minutes, both of them slacked into a mindless daze, aware of nothing but a milky haze and the music of the spheres.

14

Fargo was just drifting into sleep, a few hours after his strange encounter with Jenny, when the curtains over the doorway parted, light spilling in from the hallway.

"Skye," came Jasmine's nervous voice from the doorway, "she wants to see you and Buckshot in the kitchen. And she's fit to be tied."

"Hell, Fargo," Buckshot muttered as he tugged his boots on, "mebbe she wants to do both of us in the sink this time."

"Nothing like that," Jasmine said. "Norton found something outside."

"Shit-oh-dear," Buckshot said. "It's that damn pinfire."

El Burro, a Colt in each hand, hazed them into the kitchen. The pinfire, its cylinder open and empty, lay on the table.

"It would appear," she greeted them, "that you two are wandering from pillar to post, would it not?"

Neither man understood the high-blown remark and said nothing. Red leaped into her cheeks.

"Look at you," she taunted Fargo, voice dripping contempt. "Ruggedly handsome, a virtuoso lover, the fighting prowess of a Japanese samurai—and lacking the common sense of a donkey! What has your noble 'code' been good for? Mince pie, that's what!"

Fargo ignored the pinfire. "If you wander near a point, feel free to make it."

"Rubbish! You know damn well what I'm talking about— that pathetic weapon you stashed behind the privy. I was on the verge of offering you and Mr. Brady stakes in a bonanza. I guess we can drop the pretense, can't we, that you are intelligent enough to recognize a good opportunity?"

"Good opportunity? You're laying it on thick, lady. Yeah,

it's my gun—so what? You want me to put some water on to boil?"

"Keep a civil tongue in your head, you arrogant bastard! What we did in that bedroom this evening gives you no license to address me this way."

"Jenny, you best lower your hammer and square with the facts. I've never heard of a woman being hanged in the West nor even brought to trial. But you've broken serious federal laws, and if they haul you back to the land of steady habits, you *will* end up in a penitentiary for women."

"I'll be sure to wear ashes and sackcloth after you're gone."

Fargo didn't like that last word. "You mean after I leave?"

"Clean your ears or cut your hair, long shanks. I said *gone*."

"All your threats," Fargo said, "don't change what I said. You need to go to the street called straight, and mighty damn quick."

"Save it for your memoirs, buckskins. I've seen how it is with *honest* women in the West. They work like plow horses from can to can't. By age thirty most of them have skin like the cracked leather spines of old books. Hangtown is just a start, a way for me to get the money I need."

"Need for what?"

"For speculation and investment, that's what. That's how people not born to wealth get rich. You're smart and handsome, but you're a bigger fool than God made you. You give a good day's work for a poor day's pay, and when you can no longer work you'll die. The key is to profit off the hard labor of fools like you, but it takes money to make money."

Fargo nodded. "Yeah, I've heard this line of blather before. By your way of looking at it, I'm a fool, right enough, and so is Buckshot. But you'll never put this gulch behind you, even if you manage to get out alive. All that money you made from speculation and investment will have the stink of blood and murder on it."

This barb stuck deep, and she bristled like a feist. "You're out of line, you worthless, crusading drifter! I told you—I've murdered no one nor ordered anyone to do it unless a man deserved it. You'll find no flies on me."

"What is wrong with you and what doctor told you so? You brag about being the 'mayor' of a stinking cesspool called

Hangtown—you're telling me those graveyard rats on your payroll aren't murderers? You can see the proof dangling from that gallows. In my book that makes you a murderer, too."

"Life is cheap out here," she retorted in a pointed tone. "I suppose all that dried blood in the fringes of your buckskins came from animals?"

"Killing isn't the same as murder."

"Yes, you remember that," she said cryptically.

"All right then, kill me. I've supped full of your guff. You been threatening to do it ever since your bootlicks clouted me and Buckshot on the head three days ago."

Her shoulders suddenly slumped and she said in a miserable tone, "It appears that I won't have to kill you. It looks like Lupe Cruz is going to do that tomorrow, and I'm powerless to stop him—unless, of course, you simply refuse to go along with it."

It was the first time Fargo had ever heard her use a defeated tone. He glanced at Buckshot, who gave him a perplexed look and shrugged. When she failed to elaborate, Fargo said, "We heard that jackanapes McDade earlier today. What's this all about?"

Anger surged back into her tone. "Quicksand would spit him back up! He's making his bid for control, and he thinks I'm too stupid to see it."

She quickly explained about the knife fight proposed for tomorrow afternoon in an open expanse beside the corral.

"He claims the men got it up," she concluded. "But he's a liar. Almost certainly the idea originated with that ugly little weasel Waldo Tate. I believe Butch, however, when he says the men are champing at the bit over it and have all placed bets. They're fascinated with wagering—I've even seen them pit red ants against black and bet on the outcome."

Fargo nodded. "I see which way the wind sets. McDade warned you the men will rebel if I don't fight Cruz—it'll be proof you're mollycoddling me."

"Yes, exactly. And his claim that the fight is only to draw 'first blood,' no killing, is a patent lie also. He knows Lupe cannot be beaten in a knife fight, and the point is to kill you and perhaps Burro and Norton also. Butch hates and fears them. He probably won't kill me right away—his filthy lust must be satisfied first, and besides, most of the men like me."

Anger warred with fear in her eyes. "But the power balance will shift in his favor, and the stupid brute will expect me to become his 'regular night woman,' as he phrases it, a trophy that also consolidates his control. I would rather die than let that ignorant, unwashed animal touch me."

"On the other hand," Fargo pointed out, "if I kill Lupe Cruz, this 'power balance' of yours could still change in Butch's favor. They wouldn't take too kindly to an outsider killing one of the head hounds."

"That's likely so," Buckshot put in. "But Jenny's trapped either way, and killing one of the head hounds makes our job easier, Fargo."

She looked at Fargo. "There's no question you're a tough man. But I've seen Lupe Cruz in action with that knife. And I believe that every one of those human ears on that disgusting 'necklace' of his came from a victim of his blade."

"Fargo ain't no slouch with his Arkansas toothpick," Buckshot insisted. "But this Mexican standoff business with tying their left wrists together—they cooked that up on account they seen what Skye can do if they give him room to use his legs."

"Oh, Lupe's got the advantage on me as a knife fighter," Fargo conceded. "And I figure he's had experience in fights with the wrists tied. But I once whipped a Lakota fighting in that style, and what man has done, man can do."

"But even if you could defeat him," Jenny said, "what's to keep Butch from simply gunning you down?"

"Three good reasons," Fargo said. "El Burro, Norton, and Buckshot—he's gonna have his double-ten aimed at McDade the whole time."

Two scarlet circles of anger covered her beautiful cheekbones. "Oh, I see—so you're in charge now, is that it, and I must return his weapon?"

"Lady," Buckshot cut in, "you best shit-can them highfalutin ways right now and do what Fargo says. He's the boy you need if you and them geldings of yours want to leave this gulch alive."

"After that little stump speech he just delivered about a woman's penitentiary? I'd rather take my chances here."

"Look," Fargo said, "cooperation between the five of us is the only thing that's going to save any of us. I'm not a star-packer and I never told you *I* was going to send you to prison. Me and Buckshot rode down here to settle accounts for a worker killed by your 'unholy trinity'—and we *will* settle that account."

"And doing for Lupe Cruz," Buckshot said, "is a good start on account he's one of the killers that attacked our camp."

Fargo nodded. "But, Jenny, our only other interest in this outlaw sewer is to get Jasmine and those other five prisoners to safety, so I'll make you a deal—you, Burro, and Norton join forces with us, and once we're all shut of this place, that's the end of it. You three go your way. We'll take the prisoners and go ours."

She mulled the proposition in silence for a minute. "I'm willing to take the risk of trusting you. But, Skye, killing Lupe Cruz in a knife fight . . . ?"

"It'd be easier to put socks on a rooster," he admitted. "But long odds are better than none at all."

"Agreed. But it's not just Butch and Waldo Tate remaining—there's something like thirty men in this gulch. Mostly they're worthless louts, yes, but dangerous in a pack once they turn against me."

"First we trot and then we canter. Me and Buckshot are pretty good at exterminating vermin, and it's obvious the Burro and Norton would fight the devil in hell to save you. This won't be a trip to Santa's lap, but if I can whip that Mexer tomorrow, we got a fighting chance."

For Fargo, it felt good to again feel the reassuring weight of his Arkansas toothpick in its boot sheath. It had not only saved his life from attacks by man and animal, it had dressed out game, softened hard ground under his bedroll, and served as a saw, a cooking spit, and a medical tool to dig out bullets and arrow points and to cauterize wounds. And with skill and a bit of luck, it might save his life today.

Once again the motley group of five picked their way

through the mud wallow that served as Hangtown's only street. From a grassy clearing beside the corral, now hidden behind ramshackle structures, they could hear the excited, drunken men.

"Remember," Fargo told the others, "from the moment we get there, keep your heads on a swivel. Buckshot will keep Patsy trained on McDade. Burro and Norton, you watch the rest close. And Christ sakes, don't let Waldo Tate get behind any of us. If Lupe kills me, there's a good chance you two will be next, so be ready."

"If you're killed," Jenny fretted, "we'll all be next."

"Don't underrate Buckshot," Fargo told her. "He's pulled through plenty of bad scrapes. We talked this thing through last night—he knows what to do if I'm killed. Just do what he says."

"That's not the only reason I don't want you killed," she confessed. "Despite your disgusting integrity, you're quite a likable man."

"That's just the basket talking," Fargo quipped. But she was too nervous to even register the joke.

They rounded the corner of a canvas-and-clapboard hovel and the men cheered. But it abruptly died in their throats when Buckshot brought Patsy up to level in her hip swivel, both barrels pointing at Butch McDade. The outlaw suddenly paled.

"Don't worry, Butch," Jenny assured him, somehow assuming her old confidence. "You be a good boy and you've nothing to worry about."

"What is this shit?" he demanded. "You gave this 'breed his gun back?"

"Drop dead in a ditch," Buckshot growled. "I'm still a prisoner and so is Fargo. The lady is just protecting her flanks. If you're stupid enough to jerk that shooter back, I'm sending you to hunt the white buffalo."

Fargo spotted Lupe Cruz waiting for him in the middle of the clearing. His low-crowned shako hat left most of his face in sinister shadow. He was showing off by tossing his Spanish dag twirling high into the air and catching it by the hilt every time.

"Fargo, you poor bastard!" one of the men shouted,

obviously not buying the "no killing" rule. "Lupe's gonna slice you up like five cents' worth of liver!"

"He's gonna cut out your heart and feed it to your ass-hole!" another shouted.

"My money's on the Arkansas toothpick!" someone else roared out, and Fargo was heartened to know that even among these desperados he had his supporters. Nonetheless, nervous fear was a tight knot in his abdomen. Against a blade-runner like Lupe Cruz, there was no room for error—in a fractional second, the wrong move would spell Fargo's hard death.

"All right, boys!" Butch McDade shouted, still glowering at Buckshot. "It's gonna be a Mexican standoff! Waldo's gonna tie Lupe and Fargo's left wrists together. They start out with their knives raised straight over their heads. When Little Britches says go, they get to it. First man to draw blood wins."

He smiled slyly at Jenny before adding, "No kills. The first cut that bleeds ends it."

Lupe Cruz gave Fargo a goading smile as Tate tied their wrists. "You know how it really is, uh?" he muttered. "My blade always kills."

"The stench blowing off you, pepper gut," Fargo replied, "is likely to do me in first."

"'S'matter, Fargo?" McDade called out. "You look a little peaked. I guess your big reputation don't cut no ice in Hang-town. And facing off against Lupe Cruz ain't as much fun as bird-dogging Jenny, huh?"

"Your mouth runs six ways to Sunday, McDade," Fargo retorted. "Jenny, what say we open the ball?"

Both men raised their knives straight overhead. Fargo knew the first second was critical to his survival. If he simply tried to drop his knife hand and stick Cruz first, Fargo was gone beaver. He knew that Cruz was lightning fast and in his element. Instead, Fargo had to play to his own strength, which *was* strength—in that first eyeblink of time he had to get his right arm under Lupe's and lock it back. The rest he would figure out moment by moment, but that first move was either his salvation or his epitaph.

"Now!" Jenny shouted, and a cheer exploded from the men.

Fargo moved his right arm, swift as a striking snake, to the left and downward at a slant, successfully trapping Lupe's.

"Ah, he wishes to die slowly," Cruz goaded him, grunting with the effort to slide his knife around Fargo's arm. But the Trailsman held it back as far as possible, giving his opponent no room to maneuver.

"Fear freezes you, uh?" the Mexican taunted him. "And does she squat to piss, too?"

Lupe, well aware that Fargo could still use those powerful legs to drive a knee into his groin, maneuvered slightly sideways to protect himself.

Slowly the two men circled, each trying to figure out his next play.

"Fargo," Lupe said, playing to the crowd, "do you know that I fucked your mother?"

"That means you had to take your dick out of the chicken, right?"

The drunken men roared appreciatively, a few mocking Lupe. This loss of face clearly rattled the Mexican, but he recovered his show of bravado and nodded at Fargo.

"Good one, gringo. It is *una lastima*, a pity, that your sense of humor must die with you, uh?"

Suddenly Lupe hooked a foot behind Fargo's ankle and tried to trip him. For a moment as he recovered, Fargo was forced to lessen the pressure on Lupe's right arm. The men cheered when the Mexican almost pulled his blade free, but Fargo's catlike reflexes saved him in the nick of time as he again forced the arm back.

Cruz laughed. "*Vaya, loco!* You can delay death with your muscles, but already your arm trembles. I will be merciful and sink my steel into your warm and beating heart with one thrust. You are a worthy opponent, but you are already dead."

"Burro!" Fargo heard Jenny call out. "Waldo is trying to get behind you! Never mind watching the fight."

"And you, McDade, you whoreson shirker!" Buckshot's voice chimed in. "You keep inching your hand toward that barking iron and you're going over the mountains!"

"Have you noticed a thing, Fargo?" Lupe taunted. "Have you noticed that, when you stab a man deep, the heat from his body rushes out onto your hand?"

131

"I have," Fargo replied even as he brought his right knee up sharply. It hit Lupe's thigh instead of his groin.

So far this was truly a standoff, and the crowd was growing impatient.

"C'mon, Lupe!" one of them shouted. *"Andale, amigo!* Hurry up and kiss the mistress!"

"How do you like my necklace of ears, gringo?" Lupe goaded. "I think I will put both of yours on it. And I will make a tobacco pouch from your scrotum."

"I've always been a mite curious," Fargo riposted. "When you beaners screw your mothers, do you call them by your sister's name or your horse's?"

He finally struck pay dirt. This triple insult to Mexican manhood angered Lupe, and again he tried to trip Fargo. But this time the Trailsman was ready. When Lupe hooked a foot behind his ankle, Fargo thrust his leg to the rear hard, toppling Cruz forward and pulling both men down.

This broke Lupe's concentration for a moment, and even before they whumped hard onto the ground Fargo had dropped his right arm and driven the Arkansas toothpick deep into Lupe's vitals. Cruz emitted a shrill, almost inhuman shriek of pain as Fargo gave the blade the "Spanish twist" to ensure even more internal damage.

Fargo did indeed feel the rush of heat on his hand, followed by a sheared-copper odor of blood—warm, sticky blood that soaked the front of his shirt as the twitching, dying man lay on top him. Fargo quickly pulled his knife back out, blade shiny with gore, and sliced through the ropes binding their wrists.

He heaved the body off him, sat up, then wiped his blade off on Lupe's leg. He pushed to his feet.

"You cheating son of a bitch!" McDade exploded. "You seen it, men! Fargo was only s'pose to cut him, not kill him!"

"Don't believe this lying dog, men!" Jenny said. "It's obvious this was his plan to kill Fargo and deprive all of us of a hefty ransom. You all know that Lupe was a kill-fighter!"

Butch's face purpled with rage and he snarled like a rabid animal. Clearly he itched to gun down the unarmed Fargo on the spot, but Buckshot's double-ten was a powerful dissuasive to rash action. His trouble-seeking eyes bored into Fargo.

"Ain't *none* of you leaving this gulch, Fargo," he promised. "I'm the big he-bear now—savvy that? There'll be five more bodies hanging off that gallows."

Fargo smiled with his lips only. He kept his voice low and personal. "How's it feel, McDade?"

"How's what feel, asshole?"

"To look me in the eye and know that soon—*real* soon—you'll be walking with your ancestors?"

"You don't want a call-down with me. There ain't a man in this territory faster than me."

"Nor a knife fighter better than Lupe Cruz, right?"

"Your clover was deep, that's all. And luck don't last a lifetime unless a man dies young."

Fargo's unwavering lake blue eyes held McDade's stare until the latter finally averted his gaze.

"There'll be a call-down," Fargo assured him. "Next time you see me, I'll be heeled. You've got my ironclad guarantee on that."

15

Fargo met Jenny's eyes and gave a slight nod. The five of them had already worked out their plan of retreat from this dangerous gathering.

Most of the men were drunk and confused and posed no immediate threat unless McDade rallied them and issued orders. So Buckshot, walking backward, kept Patsy leveled on him as the group headed toward the street.

"You best keep that thumb-buster holstered," he ordered McDade. "I'm on both triggers and there ain't no slack left."

"Say, Little Britches!" one of the snowbirds wearing cavalry trousers sang out. "What the hell's going on? Are you siding with them two against us?"

"Cliff, I've always been with you boys," she replied. "The problem is Butch and that dope fiend Waldo. They plan to take over and make me their personal whore while *they* run Hangtown. Butch told me that himself just yesterday. What you see now is a woman defending herself the only way she can."

"She's a filthy, lying slut!" McDade retorted, following them into the street. "She's telling it hindside foremost! You just seen Fargo break the rules and kill Lupe, din'tcha? Next she means to have her new buck kill me and Waldo. Then her and Fargo are gonna light a shuck outta here and take all the money with 'em!"

"Remember, you two," Fargo muttered to El Burro and Norton. "As soon as Buckshot is out of range with that scattergun, McDade means to clear leather and cut us all down. Jenny assures me he's a dead shot with a six-gun. So when I give the word, Norton hands one of his Colts to Buckshot and Burro gives one of his to me. All four of us will pour lead on him while Jenny runs to the house. When your wheels are empty, haul ass yourselves. But first we've *got* to pin him down."

Another twenty yards of hair-trigger tension and then Buckshot said, "Get ready for the set-to. He's out of range for Patsy. Let's pepper that yellow cur, lads."

Jenny, catching up her skirts, began running as quickly as she could in the muck. Fargo's first shot, bullet drifting a few inches high at this range, sent McDade's hat spinning from his head. He kissed the dirt instantly as a fusillade of rounds rained in all around him.

Gray-white powder smoke hazed the street as the four men retreated backward. Most of the men in the clearing were out of sight now behind the buildings, but a few of them, armed with rifles and inspired by Dutch courage, edged around into view and opened fire.

Their guns empty, the four men broke in headlong retreat as rounds snapped past their ears and kicked up geysers of mud. Jenny made it to safety ahead of them and held the door as they bolted into the house. As planned, Jasmine had the Henry and the North & Savage ready in the hallway.

Fargo and Buckshot knelt to either side of the door and tossed their long guns into their shoulder sockets, unleashing a hot wall of lead that immediately turned back the few men who had begun surging up the street.

"The fat's in the fire now," Fargo said grimly, closing the door and dropping the bar across it. "We have to put this gulch behind us fast. The longer we hang around, the deeper we dig our own graves."

"I know this bunch," Jenny said. "They'll all congregate in the Bucket of Blood to get liquored up while Butch rallies them—he's good at firing up the men. Waldo is the brain, but he's the mouthpiece."

"Our big problem is preventing a siege of the house," Fargo said. "With the numbers against us, if they trap us here they can wait us out. We've got no horses to hand."

"Leastways they can't burn us out," Buckshot said. "This place is solid limestone and the walls are loop-holed for firing and spying out. Jenny, have they got black powder to blast us out?"

She nodded glumly. "I'm afraid so. That squat building made of logs chinked with mud, just past the Temple of Morpheus, is a powder magazine. I don't know how much is inside it, but it's the spoils of a raid on a supply caravan."

"That means we have to keep them on the defensive," Fargo said. "That's the main mile right now—we take the attack to them any way we can and keep them rattled so they can't carry out a plan. And we can't let this thing turn into a siege. Eventually we'll run out of food and ammo, and then we'll all be up Salt River."

Jenny took each man by the arm. "The supply situation is not so desperate as you think. Come see this."

She led them into the room where El Burro and Norton slept. Both men gaped in astonishment. Two army cots were pressed against one wall while most of the room was filled with neat stacks of supplies: airtights of food, cans of coal oil, cases of Volcanic and Spencer repeating rifles, boxes of ammo, various tools, even a large crate containing a Parrot muzzle-loading artillery rifle. It fired one-pound exploding shells, a case of twelve stacked next to it.

Fargo whistled. "Damn, lady! Right now I'm mighty glad you run a ring of thieves."

"So you see, we *can* hold out for a long siege."

"Nix on that," Fargo said adamantly. "This stuff will be mighty useful, all right. But like I said, we can't let this deal drag out. If we hunker down here we're just buying time, not winning the fight. Straight ahead and keep up the strut."

"But how?" Jenny demanded. "You know the numbers."

"I been studying on that. Before we do anything, we have to get those prisoners up here in the house with us. That means we have to wait until dark. There's only one guard."

"What if they increase the guard now?"

"Don't seem likely," Fargo gainsaid. "At least, not right off. McDade won't expect us to give a damn about the prisoners—he figures we'll just try to save our own bacon. And as soon as the prisoners are safe"—Fargo tapped a can of coal oil with the toe of his boot—"me and Buckshot are going to burn off all that brush surrounding the gulch."

Jenny gave him a puzzleheaded look. "But why bother, Skye?"

"It's excellent cover for them—that's why. Without it, they'll have to show themselves to attack the house. And then we can pick them off like lice from a blanket. Burro!"

The big mestizo was watching from the arched doorway. Clearly he disliked Fargo and didn't like the fact that Jenny was no longer the ramrod. Reluctantly, he turned his flat, expressionless face toward Fargo.

"You did a good job rigging up those pulleys in Jenny's room—think you can put this artillery gun together?"

"Easily," Jenny answered for the nonresponsive bodyguard.

"Assemble it out in the hallway," Fargo said, "with the muzzle aimed toward the front door. Open the crate of shells and put them next to it. Norton, get outside right now and dig a rifle pit behind the house. Make it deep and put a couple of those Volcanic rifles inside it. Place the hole so's you have a good view behind and to both sides of the house. They've got plenty of black powder, so keep a sharp eye out for anybody trying to blast the house."

Fargo mulled it for a minute and added, "After sundown, you won't be able to see much, Norton. So climb up onto the roof. Wear dark clothes and blacken your face good with gunpowder. Me and Buckshot will be burning off that brush and then you'll have a good view. But cover your ampersand up there—stay flat. If you have to open fire, make sure you keep rolling to new positions so they can't target your muzzle flash."

Both of Jenny's loyal guards clearly resented Fargo's take-charge manner. Jenny spoke up. "Boys, I hate to say it, but right now Skye Fargo speaks for me. His orders are mine. All right?"

Looking none too happy about it, both men nodded. Fargo glanced at the women. "Both of you know how to fire a rifle?"

"If it uses self-contained cartridges," Jenny said.

"Same here," Jasmine said.

"Good. Carry one at all times, and try to stay in the hallway as much as you can—it's the safest part of the house if there's an explosion. The Burro will be with you after me and Buckshot leave tonight."

"You really think we can escape this gulch, Skye?" Jasmine asked in a small, frightened voice.

Fargo flashed her a grin. "Hell, this is chicken-fixin's. Just stay frosty and remember we're up against a pack of cowards, not men fighting for a cause."

Fargo didn't add, however, the grim truth about these outlaws: just like the border ruffians in Kansas and Missouri, they were a small army, not a small gang, and in large numbers the pack mentality made even cowards dangerous.

The nighttime wind shrieked and howled like damned souls in torment. A scud of clouds blew away from the moon, and Fargo could see the guardhouse faintly below him. He and Buckshot hugged the lip of the gulch.

"Still just the one guard out front," he whispered to Buckshot. "But we'll have to put the quietus on him before he can raise the alarm."

"Gettin' here from topside was easy," Buckshot replied. "But them prisoners ain't in no shape to climb outta the gulch. We'll hafta get them to Jenny's house using the street."

"It's empty right now," Fargo pointed out. "You can hear the hell-raising from the saloon tent. They know we got no horses, and I see several guards around the corral. McDade figures we're trapped—nobody's stupid enough to try escaping on foot in this country. If we work quick and quiet, we can get those prisoners out. I'll lead, once we get them, and you and Patsy take the rearguard. Let's get it done."

A sudden wind gust almost snatched off Fargo's hat. Jasmine had washed the blood out of his buckskin shirt earlier, but it hadn't dried completely. The wind seemed to knife through it, chilling him to the bone.

Both men scrambled down into the gulch, each advancing forward along opposite sides of the crude stone guardhouse. Fargo made it to the front right corner and peered around it. The guard sat on an empty wooden barrel, an old Kentucky over-and-under rifle balanced across his thighs.

Fargo grounded his Henry. The entire gulch was strewn with rocks. He felt the ground around him until he found one that fit his hand just right. Fargo took a few moments to calculate the trajectory, then cocked his arm back and threw the rock hard.

There was a dull thud of impact, a surprised grunt, a

clatter as the rifle fell to the ground when the sentry slid off the barrel and landed in a sprawling heap.

Buckshot spurted forward, bowie knife to hand, and ended any threat of warning by slashing the outlaw's throat. Fargo ducked inside the guardhouse, which was as dark as a coal bin at midnight.

He accidentally kicked someone's leg and there was a surprised bleat of alarm.

"Hush down!" Fargo called out in a harsh whisper. "This is a rescue. You folks are going to follow me to the house at the end of the gulch. Stick behind me in single file and do exactly what I tell you."

"Oh, thank God!" a woman's voice said on a sob. "I was afraid—"

"Never mind all that," Fargo rebuked her. "Just stay quiet and follow me."

The first one to emerge behind him into the pale moonlight was the distinguished-looking middle-aged man. He froze when he saw the fresh corpse on the ground, its gaping throat still streaming blood.

"You bolted to the ground?" Fargo muttered. "Get a wiggle on, mister."

He pushed the man gently toward the street, counting as the rest emerged: five total including the mother with her baby girl.

Fargo kept them in the shadows while Buckshot brought up the rear, walking backward and keeping his double-ten at the ready. Fargo kept throwing glances over his shoulder. Abruptly, a man staggered out of the tent saloon.

"Everybody stoop down," Fargo ordered, fearing they had been discovered. But the man, clearly drunk as Davy's saw, drew his short iron and fired all six rounds at the moon. Then he howled like a banshee and staggered back into the tent.

They made it to the house without incident. Fargo called through the door and the Burro threw it open. Jasmine hurried forward to assist the older woman, who was unsteady on her feet.

Fargo said, "Jasmine, rustle up some grub and coffee for these folks. I saw canned milk among the supplies. Warm some up for this baby."

"How will we get it in her? We have no pap boat."

"I have a gravy boat with a long spout," Jenny said. "If you're careful, that will work."

Fargo looked at the small child's pale, sickly face in the glow of the hallway candles. The young mother's dirty face was drawn and lined deep with worry. Then he stared at Jenny.

"Ain't you proud?" he said, his voice heavy with disgust. "You knew that little girl needed milk, her ma said so. Yet you never offered it."

Her face hardened against him. "Go to hell, Pastor Fargo. I forgot it was there. I don't rake through those supplies every day."

Fargo turned away and looked at Buckshot. "Well, I didn't get you killed that time out, old son. Let's grab a couple cans of coal oil and see if I don't have better luck this time. We got a brush fire to start, and the way that wind's kicking up, it oughta be a humdinger."

16

Despite recent rains the thick brush ringing the gulch was dry from the hot, parched summer months and made for excellent tinder. Fargo and Buckshot fashioned two crude torches by breaking a broom handle in half and tying rags to the ends.

"When we finish up splashing the brush," Fargo said, "be sure to save a little coal oil to soak your rag. We'll start at this end laying down the oil, then start at the other end lighting it. Even drunk as those shit-heels are by now, they'll notice the flames quick enough. So we want to be moving toward the house, not away from it."

The two men had hauled five-gallon cans of coal oil into the hallway and had just finished making the torches. Jasmine was feeding the freed prisoners in the kitchen. Earlier El Burro had successfully assembled the Parrot artillery rifle, and now it rested on its tripod near the front door, leaving just enough space in the hallway to squeeze around it.

"I been cogitatin'," Buckshot said. "Why'n't we splash that powder magazine while we're at it, set it ablaze? The sooner the better—won't be long and they'll try to blow us to smithereens. Mebbe even tonight."

"Yeah, I thought about that, too," Fargo said. "But fire might take too long and give them time to save the powder." His gaze shifted toward the Parrot. "I got a better idea for that magazine."

"I still don't understand," Jenny cut in after listening to them, "why it's worth the risk of getting shot to burn down the brush."

"Because this is a gulch. We're trapped in the back of a box without a lid," Fargo replied.

"Back of a . . .? Do you mind speaking plainly instead of in Chinese riddles?"

"Pardon me all to hell," Fargo said sarcastically. "God knows *you're* a plain speaker, Miss 'Unconventional Predilections.' "

"T'hell with that skirt," Buckshot put in. "Ain't none of her beeswax. This is men's business we're talking. Top of all that, she's the hellcat what started all this."

"Simmer down," Fargo warned, seeing El Burro's eyes start to snap sparks. "It's too dead to skin now. Let's just all get out of here in one piece."

He added more patiently, "Jenny, you know how it is with these louts. Most of them are easy-go killers, but when it boils down to a hard fight they're all gurgle and no guts. Taking down that excellent brush cover forces them into the open—forces them to fight or show yellow. I say they'll show yellow."

She thought it over. "Yes, I take your point. Well hidden in that brush they could prevent us from escaping the 'box' you mentioned. And it would make a siege more difficult for them because they have to get close to the edges to fire on us."

"Which also makes it more likely that McDade's toadeaters will go puny on him. And less likely that you'll decide to use this place again since it's no longer hidden."

"Well, you needn't worry about that—I'll be grateful to escape this place. But don't be too certain," Jenny cautioned, "that the men will be easy to scare off. You see, I have the lion's share of the money . . . the swag, as Butch loves to call it. Nor are they eager to leave the safety of Hangtown. As squalid as it is, they prefer it to the dangerous, itinerant existence of outlaw fugitives on the run."

"Yeah, well we'll see about all that money you're hoarding," Fargo said.

Her eyes shot daggers at him. "Would you care to elaborate on that?"

"Let's stow the chin-wag," Buckshot snapped. "Them scurvy-ridden sons-a-bitches could move on us any damn time now."

"When the two men we just rescued finish eating," Fargo

142

told Jenny as he grabbed a can of coal oil, "give them each a rifle. Cover both doors, and if anybody tries to bust through, make it hot for 'em."

Fargo cautiously cracked the back door open and peered out into the moonlit night. Norton had finished digging a rifle pit, but it was empty.

"Norton," he called out, "it's Fargo. If you're on the roof, come to the back edge. But stay low so's you don't skyline yourself."

A moment later the guard's face appeared.

"See any movement along the rim of the gulch?" Fargo asked.

Norton shook his head.

"All right. We're gonna fire up the brush now. Climb on down and hand these cans up to us."

Safely up on the western rim of the gulch, Buckshot took the southern flank, Fargo the northern. The Trailsman watched for sentries as he hurried along the rim dispensing the coal oil. As he approached the eastern end, above the gallows, he could see orange-glowing cigarettes marking at least three sentries around the corral.

Fargo soaked his torch and huddled low to block the wind as he struck a phosphor to life. The torch flamed up and he began hurrying back toward the house, touching off the dry brush as he moved. The strong gusts quickly fanned the flames. Moments later the opposite rim erupted in flames too.

"Christ, boys, lookit!" one of the sentries shouted. "The brush is going up!"

Fargo was perhaps halfway back to the house when the rataplan of pursuing hooves sounded behind him. The bright flames made him an easy target, and rifles and six-guns opened up behind him, crackling almost like the flames.

However, those same flames also brightly illuminated the outlaws. Fargo turned, dropped to a kneeling offhand position, and put the Henry through its well-oiled paces, working the lever rapidly and chucking a deadly hail of lead at men and horses.

The lead rider caught a bullet in his leg and made the foolish mistake of reining left, too close to the snapping flames. His horse immediately panicked and bucked the rider into the midst of the burning brush. He screamed in agony and managed to crawl out, hair and clothing flaming in macabre outline against the night.

That sent the other riders retreating away from the flames, but by now men had poured out of the saloon tent below and opened up blindly toward the flaming rims on both sides. Fargo heard Buckshot's big North & Savage booming as he, too, made for the house.

The men firing from the street below couldn't see Fargo behind the wall of flames, but so many had opened up that a few rounds whiffed in dangerously close to him. He and Buckshot reached the rim behind the house almost simultaneously.

"Still sassy, Buckshot?"

"Sassy as the first man breathed on by God! We done stepped on the hornets' nest now, Skye. Them pukes are bilin' mad."

"Good. Pissed-off men let their emotions force them into stupid mistakes. Anyhow, we're about to make 'em a lot madder. Norton, don't shoot! Fargo and Buckshot coming in."

They scrambled down and Fargo gave the hail again at the door to avoid being cut down when they entered the house.

"Get to the front door," Fargo told Buckshot. "When I tell you, fling it open and duck aside. We're gonna take out that powder magazine before those drunken sots organize a plan. Jenny, Jasmine, stand by to snuff the hallway candles."

Fargo pulled open the loading gate at the rear of the Parrot, seated a one-pound exploding shell, closed the gate and gripped the elevation knob.

"Douse those candles!" he ordered. "Then everybody clear the hallway. Buckshot, soon as the light goes out open that door and cover down. After I pop off this round, shut it again."

The moment Buckshot shoved the door open Fargo manhandled the gun's tripod to get the muzzle in line with the log structure serving as powder magazine. Then he cranked the elevation knob a few clicks to bring the gun on bead.

He jerked the chain lanyard, the artillery rifle rocked back in its greased slide, and an earsplitting boom shook the house. An eyeblink later the entire gulch lit up like broad daylight when the powder magazine detonated in a second explosion, a blast so loud it left Fargo's ears ringing.

Buckshot leaped to shut the door. "Tumbledown Dick! That's holding and squeezing, Fargo. Say! Why stop with one little love bite? We got eleven more shells—let's just blow the whole goldang shootin' match sky high, rats, nest, and all."

"Does your mother know you're out? Those horses in the corral are already spooked from the rim fires—it's risky enough firing the one shell. We're going to need some of those horses to get these folks to safety. And to tell it straight—slaughtering men wholesale—even outlaws—don't set well with me."

"Huh! You can kill 'em all and let God sort 'em out for aught I care."

Fargo shook his head. "That risks the horses, too. If we push these men too hard and drive them out in a panic all at one time, they'll either take all the horses or scatter the ones they don't take. Use your noodle, old son."

"Yeah, all that shines. But you're the one said we need to take the fight to 'em hard and fast so's they can't organize a good plan. We got to end it or mend it, and it's way past mending. So what do we do now—stand around with our thumbs up our sitters?"

"Nope. First we're gonna cut off the head of the snake and see if that ends it."

"Jenny's right as rain 'bout you and Chinee riddles. The hell you talking about?"

"Butch McDade, jughead—who else? Earlier today I promised him a throw-down, remember? And I'm a man likes to keep his promises."

On the morning of the ninth day after the attack on Ed Creighton's work crew, smoke hazed Hangtown as the ruins of the powder magazine still smoldered along with the hot ashes where the brush once concealed the gulch.

A half dozen men had quietly slipped out during the night, and Butch McDade realized the fever had reached its crisis. The men's faith in his leadership was crumbling fast, and he knew that if he didn't act quickly and decisively, his cake was dough.

Soon after sunrise a man was sent to gather the remaining outlaws for a meeting in the Bucket of Blood. As the disgruntled and hungover outlaws filed in, McDade and Waldo Tate conferred at one end of the plank bar.

"Butch, this deal looks bad," Waldo said quietly. "More of the men will dust their hocks today if we don't kill Fargo and that half-breed."

"Where you been grazing?" Butch snapped, tossing back a jolt of Indian burner. "That's old news. Tell me something useful, you rat-faced twat."

Butch stood with his hands balled on his hips, his breathing ragged, his shoulders hunched as if to ward off wind. "Fargo's clover is deep, that's all," he said as if trying to convince himself.

"Clover? Butch, you said the same thing yesterday when he gutted Lupe. Luck's not got thing one to do with it—he's not just some got-up, nickel-novel hero like you've been claiming. Lupe ain't all of it. Look at what he's done already to Hangtown in just one night, and how Fargo and that half-breed siding him escaped from us the first day we spotted them. The man is all he's cracked up to be."

"Yeah? Sounds like you wanna kiss his ass. I'm telling you he's shit! You notice how he's avoiding a call-down with me after that bluff of his yesterday?"

"Maybe he is sane enough to avoid a call-down with you, but he's still got the whip hand."

But Butch wasn't listening. "It's that goddamn, double-crossing Little Britches, Waldo! She used her little cunny to hook Fargo. She's got most of the legem pone, and she's splitting our share with Fargo."

"Butch, never mind Little—"

"Never mind a cat's tail, you little ferret! Go smoke you another tar ball and get some more big ideas like that knife fight."

Butch stewed some more and his face turned choleric with rage. "It's the bitch, I'm telling you! Acts like she's one of the Quality—oh, *her* shit don't stink! Well, mister, she gave Butch McDade the rough side of her tongue one time too many. I'm gonna let every swinging dick in this gulch bull her, and then I'm gonna feed her liver to the dogs."

Waldo gripped Butch's beefy shoulder. "Snap out of it! You've been arguing full bore about how we have to settle Fargo's hash. Now you're harping on Jenny. Butch, just admit it—Fargo has put ice in your boots."

Butch snarled and knocked the hand away. His booming voice rose in anger. "Ease off that talk, Waldo, or you'll be getting your mail delivered by moles. It's *Fargo* who's got icy boots. He's yellow! All I ask is for a call-down with that lanky, woman-stealing bastard, that's all."

"All right, Butch," said a calm, commanding voice from the open fly of the tent. "Let's get thrashing."

17

Every man in the Bucket of Blood had riveted his attention on the unfolding argument between Butch McDade and Waldo Tate. No one had noticed the two imposing figures now filling the entrance.

At the sound of Fargo's voice, McDade froze like a hound on point. Waldo, however, immediately turned away and lost himself among the other men.

Fargo's Henry was at sling-arms around his left shoulder. Buckshot held Patsy at the ready, watching the assembly with hawk eyes that stayed in constant motion. He remained in the entrance when Fargo took a few steps inside.

"Sounds like you're a big he-bear on the scrap," Fargo said amiably. "Me, I'm the kind of hombre likes to accommodate a jasper who's eager for a frolic. You *are* eager for a frolic, ain't you, Butchie Boy?"

Butch finally looked at him, his face twisted with insolence. "Fargo, you're a damn fool. You see how many armed men are in this tent? You just strolled right into the lion's den."

"That's the only way to beard him. So I'm yellow *and* a fool? I'll give you the fool part—every man has a fool up his sleeve now and again. But by 'yellow' do you mean that I have a liver condition?"

Butch averted his eyes. "I think you know what it means."

"I do, yeah. But I guess it don't matter how much you insult me now—I came here to kill you, and since a man can only die once, you can have at me all you want. It's the least I can do for a blowhard, white-livered, murdering son of a bitch who's seen his last sunrise."

A few men looked restless and on the verge of some action. Buckshot noticed this and spoke up.

"My name is Buckshot Brady, and this here is my gal Patsy Plumb. I learned my lore from the Taos Trappers, Kit Carson, and Uncle Dick Wootton, and I am a voracious, man-killing son of a bitch! I've kilt Utes, Apaches, Sioux, Crows, Cheyennes, Mexers, dagos, frogs, limeys, and that's just my Sunday list. I'm plumb savagerous and mean when my dander is up, and the first one a you little sissy bitches what goes for her gun"—here Buckshot wagged the barrel of his double-ten—"is gonna get a meat-bag fulla blue whistlers."

"Don't let that mouthy 'breed buffalo you, boys," McDade said in a tight, nervous voice. "Nor Fargo neither. We got the numbers on 'em!"

"Seems to me, Butchie Boy," Fargo said, "like you're trying to weasel out of that call-down you wanted so bad. Never mind them—this is *our* waltz."

"You got no dicker with me, Fargo. I ain't never done nothing to you."

"Opinions vary on that. I count at least three times you tried to get my life over. One up north in a cowardly ambush; the second time six days ago when I first rode into these parts; the third time yesterday when your greaser buddy tried to add my ears to his necklace. But it was a fellow named Danny Appling who sent me down here."

"Hell, I don't know nobody by that name."

Fargo nodded, smiling his smile that wasn't really a smile. "You don't know his widow or kids, neither, but you killed him just the same. Cut him down in cold blood. That account has to be settled."

"Christ, man, there was three of us rode up there. How do you know which one of us—"

"It's all one." Fargo cut him off. "A fish rots from the top, and that raid was your idea. You sowed the wind, and now you'll reap the whirlwind."

While all this went forward, Waldo Tate had discreetly been moving through the crowd of men, angling behind Fargo. Buckshot had seen him, too. The moment Waldo's hand tickled his canvas holster, Buckshot shouted, "H'ar now! You men standing next to or behind that back-shooter Waldo Tate best make a big hole around him on account I aim to put one *through* him."

The men cleared away from Tate as if he carried plague.

Waldo went pale as new gypsum. "Now, just hold your horses, Brady! My hand to God, I was only—"

"Chuck the flap-jaw, you egg-sucking groat. I seen what you was up to."

"You can't just gun me down, man!"

"Fargo wouldn't, maybe. He's a *noble* son of a bitch, and he'd likely give you an even chance. Me, I'm just a stone cold, mother-lovin' killer."

"I got gold, Brady, plenty of it! I can make you rich! I—"

Buckshot thumbed one hammer back with a menacing click, and Waldo fell silent abruptly as if he'd been slugged.

"You're a back-shooting coward," Buckshot pronounced in his gravelly voice. "Danny was just workin' hard to feed his family when you scum buckets burned him down. Then you three bushwhackers turned your guns on me and Fargo."

"He ain't stupid enough to kill you, Waldo," Butch scoffed. "He knows his ass is grass if he does."

"Yeah," Waldo said, grasping at this straw, "you best think about it because—"

Patsy's right muzzle spat flame and double-aught buckshot, the blast deafening inside the tent. Tate's entrails splatted in a greasy spray onto the wall of the tent behind him, his corpse flying head-over-handcart. Before the men could recover from their shock, Buckshot broke open the breach and inserted a shell into the empty chamber.

"Good God-a-gorry!" someone exclaimed.

"That's two down, Butchie Boy," Fargo said, his eyes hard as blue gems now. "You're the last one. Get coiled and throw down."

"Now, just a goddamn minute here, Fargo," McDade blustered. "You're on *my* range now. I don't hafta—"

"Shut your filthy sewer and keep it shut. I'm making the medicine around here and you're taking it. You just made your brag how you wanted a draw-shoot with me. So here's your big chance to make your boys proud—quit mealy-mouthing and throw down."

"Nerve up, damn it, alla yous!" Butch shouted to his men.

"The hell you waiting for? We got the numbers on these bastards—smoke them down!"

"Fargo's right," spoke up Cliff, the snowbird who had challenged Jenny at the knife fight yesterday. "You got it bass-ackward, Butch. You're the one's been spoiling for a cartridge session with Fargo, not us. Well, there he stands."

"Throw down," Fargo repeated.

"Holy Hannah!" someone exclaimed. "Butch just pissed himself!"

"Jerk it back," Fargo ordered. "This is the final reckoning, McDade."

As if finally realizing cowardice wouldn't save his bacon, a transformation came over McDade's brutally handsome face. Determined confidence washed out the craven fear, for after all McDade had every right to trust in his skills as a shootist. That skill had left a trail of graves from Missouri to California, and besides, for all his notoriety, Skye Fargo was not ballyhooed as a gunslinger. All the guts in the world couldn't trump superior speed in the draw.

"All right, crusader," he replied, pushing away from the plank bar and coiling, "I been packing heaven full of fresh souls for a long time, but there's always room for one more."

A slight movement of McDade's neck muscles was all the warning Fargo needed. *Here's the fandango,* he told himself just before McDade made his play and Fargo filled his fist with blue steel.

It was over in a few thundering heartbeats, but for Fargo the critical moments of life-or-death action always had a dreamlike slowness to them as if they were happening underwater. He became both participant and observer simultaneously.

The observer in him realized, heart sinking, that Butch McDade was faster, his walnut-gripped Remington clearing leather an eyeblink before Fargo's Colt. But the participant in him remained confident and sure of purpose when a nerve-rattled McDade bucked his trigger, the bullet tracking wide and taking a couple of fringes off Fargo's shirt.

The participant knew, instinctively, that the easy, center-of-mass shot might allow McDade a second chance to score a kill. Instead, Fargo drilled a slug through McDade's forehead and into his brain. Unlike in the melodramatic fiction of the Wild West, McDade did not fling his arms wide and stagger a few steps forward. He simply flopped straight down as if his bones had turned to water, toes scratching a few times as his nervous system protested its sudden destruction.

Wisps of smoke still snake-danced from the Colt's muzzle as Fargo leathered his shooter. The men in the tent stood as still as pillars of salt, staring at their dead leader.

"Boys," Fargo announced, "I'm one to take the easy way when I can, but I'll keep up the killing way if that's what you choose. Face it—it's all over for Hangtown. That fire last night—I'll guarandamntee that red aborigines somewhere saw it, and they'll be riding here soon to see what gives. The paleface can usually travel across their land, but they draw the line at settlements of any kind. And with the ring of brush gone, they *will* spot this place. You hang around here too long and your dander will end up hanging from a coup stick."

Fargo let that sink in, then added, "I have a message for you from Jenny. Any man who agrees to ride out from this place by noon today gets three hundred dollars in gold and silver. That's a damn good trail stake."

"She's got more than that," a voice protested.

"She has," Fargo agreed. "But the rest will be divided up among the prisoners, who lost everything when you boys kidnapped them, and Danny Appling's widow."

Cliff hooted. "Say, I know Little Britches—*she* never came up with a plan like that. That woman is tight as Dick's hatband."

Fargo grinned. "Let's just say I helped her come to Jesus."

"I can't speak for the rest," Cliff said, "but it sounds jake to me. A bunch of us was planning on lighting a shuck out of here anyhow. These diggings are used up."

Many of the others chorused assent.

"All right," Fargo said. "You'll be paid off at the corral. But every man hops his own horse and takes only his own tack. Me and Buckshot have killed about ten of you, and the dead men's horses and leather remain behind."

"What about their weapons?"

"Take 'em."

"Hey, Fargo!" one of them called out. "Didja notice that Butch shucked out his six-gun before you did?"

Fargo glanced at the corpse. "I did. Of the two of us, he was the faster draw. But I scored the first hit, and in a gunfight that's all that really matters."

18

When playing poker Fargo trusted everybody—but he always cut the cards.

With this ragtag group of desperados he took no chances. He stood outside the corral and paid off each man as he rode out. Directly above them, commanding an excellent line of fire, stood Buckshot, El Burro, and Norton, all grim-faced and armed with rifles.

"Fargo," one of the snowbirds said as he pocketed his money and hit leather, "my name is Chilly Davis. I'm a no-'count son of a bitch and always will be. I prefer the outlaw life to bustin' sod like my pap did. But I've never murdered a man in my life, and I deliberately shot wide when we was chasing you and your pard a week ago. Before I took a sudden freak to desert the army, I was in Colonel Helzer's unit when you was chief of scouts at Fort Union. I ain't the only ex-soldier among us who rates you mighty damn high."

Fargo reached up to shake his hand when he extended it from the saddle.

"'Preciate that, Chilly. It's live and let live with me until it becomes kill or be killed. I'm glad you men decided to ease out of this deal. If you insist on riding the owlhoot trail, then at least stop the damn kidnapping. Go after the railroads and mining operations and such, not the innocents who are just struggling to get by."

Chilly pondered that and nodded. "Yeah. Little Britches is a mighty fine-looking woman, but her heart is cold as last night's mashed potatoes. We was all sorta . . . I dunno, under her spell, you might say. You think maybe she's learned a lesson out of all this?"

Fargo snorted. "I wouldn't bet a plugged peso on it."

Fargo's next priority, after the last man had ridden out, was to retrieve the Ovaro and Buckshot's grulla. He saddled an outlaw horse and headed for the draw, his stomach a knot of apprehension. It had been a day and a half since he had checked on the horses, too damn long to leave spirited stallions on a tether.

Even before he rode into the hidden draw, he heard the Ovaro whiffle in greeting. Fargo rode into view of the horses, then abruptly reined in.

"Well, I'll be shot and shanghaied," he muttered as he took in the scene.

Both horses were complacently grazing the last of the lush grass they could reach. Two dead gray wolves were drawing flies in the grass, their skulls caved in.

"Ain't you two some pumpkins?" he praised as he swung down. The Ovaro bumped Fargo's chest with his nose, glad to see him. Neither horse had a scratch on him. Those wolves, Fargo thought, should have looked elsewhere for their supper.

He fed each of them a little grain, deciding to water them after the short ride back. He tacked both mounts and put the grulla and the outlaw horse on a lead line, then swung up and over. The Ovaro, impatient to race the wind, fought the bit all the way.

When Fargo returned, El Burro and Norton were busy loading a buckboard Jenny had kept in the corral. Buckshot and Tim Landry, the young father who had just been rescued, had already tacked five horses for the trail and tied the rest on a line.

"Mr. Fargo," Landry said with heartfelt feeling as Fargo lit down, "I ain't got the words to tell you and Buckshot how beholden all of us are. Without you two we didn't have a Chinaman's chance. If that Jenny Lavoy was a man, I'd baste her bacon for what she done to us. She didn't have any plans for returning us once ransoms were paid—I heard her men talking about it. She saw little Sarah suffering bad and didn't do a damn thing about it."

"How is the little girl?" Fargo asked.

Landry perked up. "Why, she already looks better since she's had some milk. She even giggled some this morning.

Pretty soon Katherine will get her strength back and be able to nurse the baby proper on ma's milk."

"I already rigged up a soft backboard for the baby," Buckshot said. "We'll go turnabout and carry her just like a papoose. Jasmine's just finished making a little sun bonnet for her."

"Where do you think the six of us should go?" Landry asked. "Fort Laramie?"

Fargo shook his head. "Nix on that. It's too far to the east and you folks would be on your own. I got a better plan. It will delay your arrival in Oregon, but at least you'll be headed west again. I want all six of you to join Ed Creighton's work crew and stick with us to Fort Bridger in Utah. With the money Jenny paid you, you'll be able to afford the stage fare from there. Mormon soldiers escort all the stage runs, so you'll be well protected."

"Say! That plan's a humdinger, all right. But . . . will Mr. Creighton be willing to take six of us under his wing—and with a little baby and all?"

Fargo chuckled. "You needn't fret being unwelcome. Half the men on his crew are young fathers with little tads of their own, and they *will* spoil that little girl."

"They'll all be happy as pigs in mud to have Jasmine around, too," Buckshot added slyly.

Fargo grinned. "Yeah, might even catch her a husband. As for Big Ed, he's a gruff old rooster at times, but the milk of human kindness flows in his veins, and he'll insist you folks stay with them. He'll prob'ly try to hire you on, though, Tim. You look like a sturdy fellow and he's short on workers. The job ain't so hard and the wages are fair."

"Then I'm his man—I was a rail-splitter back in Iowa, and hard work is the street I live on."

"Well, isn't this a cozy little scene?" came a sarcastic voice from the doorway behind them.

Fargo turned around and felt his face drain cold—Jenny stood in the doorway with her over-and-under hideout gun aimed at him.

"Fargo, do you realize how much you've cost me? I can barely rub two nickels together, thanks to your forced settlement with the outlaws and these prisoners. Almost a year of hard work and careful planning, all up in smoke, thanks to your sanctimonious meddling."

"Why, you treacherous little hussy," Buckshot said, anger spiking his voice.

Fargo, however, looked closely into those fetching brown eyes and spotted a mischievous twinkle. He laughed.

"Ease off the trigger, old bird dog," he told Buckshot, who was on the verge of swinging Patsy up. "No need to get your pennies in a bunch—she's just playing the larks with us."

"Save your breath to cool your porridge, you damn fool! Playing the larks, huh? Is that why that shooter of hers is aimed right at your cod?"

"She's not that stupid," Fargo said even as Jenny grinned wickedly and dropped the weapon into a skirt pocket. "If she meant to burn us down, she'd have the Burro and Norton backing her play—and she'd use a gun with more than two bullets in it."

"Yes, I just wanted to see Fargo squirm," she admitted. "I hate to say it, but I'm grateful to you two trail bummers. My situation here was untenable, and you've saved my life if not my treasure."

"'Untenable.'" Buckshot spat the word out as if it had a nasty taste. "You and them damn thirty-five-cent words."

"Decided where you three are going?" Fargo asked her.

"Yes, due south to Santa Fe. I hear there's an abundance of rich men there with money to burn, so I'm going to help them burn it."

Tim Landry had been biting his tongue. "Well, I for one hope Indians scalp and torture all three of you along the way. You are an evil woman."

She glanced at him with little interest. "Yes, I certainly am," she replied demurely. "That's why I sleep between silk sheets while you huddle under horse blankets."

"Never mind all that," Fargo snapped. "Tim, I made a deal with her and I have to keep my word and let her go. Let's get horsed and clear out of here before we *all* get an Indian haircut. I'd wager a war party is headed this way after that fire last night."

"One moment, Mr. Fargo," Jenny said. "Mr. Landry has

raised the subject of simmering resentments—you promised Burro that you were going to kill him for beating you while your hands were tied. Do you still mean that?"

Fargo glanced at the big mestizo. "Nah. I was a mite steamed at the time. You don't kill a man for hitting you, I reckon. I'll settle for this."

Fargo bridged the gap in three quick paces and threw a hard right punch to El Burro's face. A moment later, Fargo was hopping around in a little circle, clutching his right hand and cursing like a stable sergeant.

"Son of a *bitch*! Did I miss and hit the house?"

This display threw Buckshot into stitches. He laughed so hard he had to grab the buckboard to steady himself. "Fargo, you consarn idiot! The mighty Trailsman . . . why'n't you piss into the wind while you're at it?"

Fargo met the Burro's unfathomable dark eyes. The man was completely unfazed by the punch. For the first and only time, he gave Fargo a little twitch of a grin.

"Jenny," Fargo said, still embarrassed, "call the others out of the house. It's time to raise dust."

The men helped Jasmine, Katherine Landry, and Louise Fredericks, the middle-aged matron from Boston, into their saddles. But one important task remained.

"Buckshot," he said, "let's load those last eleven artillery shells into the buckboard. Then we're gonna drag the gun outside and tie it to the tailgate."

"Have you taken leave of your senses?" Jenny demanded. "These horses have enough weight to—"

"Simmer down," Fargo interrupted her. "They're only gonna drag it to the head of the gulch."

Fargo watched El Burro swing into a fancy silver-trimmed Mexican saddle. He admired the strong-looking claybank the Burro had selected.

"That was Butch McDade's horse," Jenny explained, seeing Fargo admire it. "And the blood bay Norton's riding was Lupe Cruz's. I only hope they aren't as mean and nasty as their former masters."

"Oh, I'm sure you'll gentle them," Fargo quipped before he and Buckshot went back into the house.

Twenty minutes later, after the horses had tanked up at

the corral trough, the Parrot rifle sat on a little rise about fifty yards back from the entrance to the gulch.

"What are you doing, Skye?" a curious Jasmine asked as Fargo loaded the first exploding shell.

"Making sure nobody else is tempted to set up a robbers' roost here," Fargo said. "I'm damned if I want to clean it out again."

Fargo yanked the lanyard and continued loading and firing repeatedly, walking the shells down both sides of the mud wallow. He sent the gallows, the corral, the Temple of Morpheus, the Bucket of Blood and the stone guardhouse into oblivion in a series of crack-booming explosions. The resulting fires quickly spread through the tar-paper shacks and shebangs.

"Hookey Walker!" Buckshot exclaimed. "Lookit all the damn rats escaping!"

Fargo had saved two shells for the solid limestone structure at the far end of the gulch. No doubt it had served its purpose well as a secure winter quarters for fur traders many years ago, but as Jenny Lavoy had proved in spades, it was also an ideal bastion for criminals.

The first shell only damaged the place; the second brought it crumbling in on itself in a huffing cloud of dust and debris.

"Oh, my beautiful furnishings," Jenny lamented.

"Your beautiful *stolen* furnishings," Fargo corrected her.

"Yes, Pastor Fargo," she replied, but with no venom in her tone this time, "my stolen furnishings. But I did save one item."

Smiling conspiratorially at him, she pivoted on the seat and lifted one corner of an eiderdown quilt covering the loaded buckboard. Fargo felt his lips tugging into a grin.

Her specially constructed basket, complete with the system of pulleys.

"Next time you drift into Santa Fe," she added, "please look me up. I very much enjoyed . . . hanging around you."

Fargo's grin stretched itself wider. "I just might, at that. I got nothing against working under a woman."

"I just couldn't leave it behind. In all your vast amorous experience," she asked him, "can you honestly say you recall anything more . . . unique?"

Fargo expelled a long sigh. By rights he ought to hate this woman with a white-hot intensity. The suffering she had caused was beyond calculation, and even now she was blithely unrepentant.

But some hard-to-define quality about Jenny Lavoy, a vital essence beyond language, made it impossible for him to hate her. He disliked these moments of moral ambiguity, but after all, he had doubtless done more than any other man to resist and control her. If human sympathy had its limits, so, too, did his capacity for judging women as harshly as he did men.

"No, lady," he finally replied, "I cannot. You are definitely an American original."

Fargo took one last gander at the smoking, flaming ruins of a literal rat's nest that had almost become the end of his last trail. Then he shook off his pensive mood and looked at Buckshot.

"All right, old son, let's fork leather and point our bridles north."

LOOKING FORWARD!
The following is the opening section of the next novel in the exciting *Trailsman* series from Signet:

TRAILSMAN #380
TEXAS TORNADO

Texas, 1861—a town wants to clap Fargo in leg irons, but they'll do it over his dead body.

The baying of hounds keened in the hot, muggy air of a Texas afternoon.

Skye Fargo drew rein to listen. A big man, broad at the shoulder, slender at the hips, he wore buckskins and a white hat brown with dust. A red bandanna around his neck lent a splash of color. In a holster nestled a Colt that had seen a lot of use, and snug in a boot, hidden from prying eyes, was an Arkansas toothpick. The stock of a Henry rifle jutted from his saddle scabbard.

The baying grew louder.

He figured a hunter was after game. Maybe a deer, maybe an antelope, although dogs had little hope of catching one.

Fargo was in a part of Texas he had never been to before, a sea of grassy plain broken here and there by rolling hills. Comanches roamed there and killed any whites they came across. That hadn't stopped the white man, though, from establishing settlements and even a few towns.

Judging by the tracks and wagon ruts Fargo had come across, there was one up ahead. He reckoned to stop and treat himself to a few drinks before pushing on.

From the crest of a low hill, he could see for half a mile or more out across the plain. His lake blue eyes narrowed when he caught sight of a lone figure running in his direction. The animal the hounds were after, he reckoned.

Then he realized the figure was on two legs, not four.

Fargo stayed put. Long ago he'd learned not to stick his nose into affairs that didn't concern him.

The figure came on fast but not fast enough. The hounds appeared, far back. They were gaining. Now and then they bayed.

"None of my concern," Fargo said to the Ovaro.

The stallion had its ears pricked and was staring intently at the unfair race.

Then Fargo glimpsed flowing brown hair, and it hit him that the figure was a woman in a shirt and britches. Just like that, everything changed. A tap of his spurs brought the stallion to a trot. He descended the hill and rode to intercept her.

The woman was losing steam. She weaved and staggered and slowed and stopped. That she had run for so long in that awful heat was remarkable. Now it was taking its toll.

Head down, she was breathing in great gasps, a hand pressed to her side. She was unaware of Fargo until he was almost on top of her.

Snapping erect, her hazel eyes filling with fear, she cried out, "No! I won't let you!"

Fargo liked what he saw. She had an oval face, lovely as could be, and an equally striking figure that her baggy shirt and loose pants couldn't conceal. He smiled and said, "I don't aim to hurt you, ma'am. Are you in some sort of trouble?"

"What?" she said, as if she hadn't heard right.

"Those dogs," Fargo said, with a nod at the approaching hounds.

"What?" she said again.

Further back, Fargo noticed, were several men on horseback.

"Oh God," she said, and hope replaced her fear. "You're not from there, are you?"

"From where?"

"Fairplay," the woman said.

"Never heard of it."

The woman glanced over her shoulder and blanched. Suddenly she came to the Ovaro and gripped Fargo's leg with surprising strength. "Please," she said. "Get me out of here."

"What's this all about?" Fargo wanted to know. "Why are those men after you?"

"I don't have time to explain." She held fast with both hands. "I'm begging you. Help me up and ride like the wind."

Fargo would have been the first to admit he had a weakness for a pretty face. He was about to lower his arm and swing her up when his gaze fell on the men on horseback. The gleam of metal on a vest gave him pause. "Are those lawmwen?"

"They're animals," the woman said. "The whole town." Tears filled her eyes and desperation her voice. "For God's sake, take me out of here before it's too late."

It already was.

The four hounds arrived in a flurry of legs and tails. The foremost, a big brute with floppy ears and a mouth brimming with teeth, made straight for the woman. Its intention was clear, and it coiled to spring.

Fargo drew and fanned a shot from the hip. He didn't shoot the dog; not when the law was involved. He fired into the ground in front of it, and the hound veered and yipped and came to a stop. So did the rest of the pack.

Fargo held the Colt ready to shoot again if the dogs came at her but they stood there growling and looking from him to her, uncertain what to do.

The three riders were at a gallop.

Turning with her back to the Ovaro, the woman let out a sob and clutched at her throat. "Oh God," she said. "Oh God, oh God, oh God."

Fargo had been right; all three riders wore tin stars.

The man in the lead had a belly that bulged over a wide

belt and a moon face that glistened with sweat. A short-brimmed hat looked too small for his big head. His pudgy right hand rested on a hip above one of a matched pair of Starr revolvers. He brought his bay to a stop and scowled. Looking at the hounds, he said, "I thought you shot one, mister."

Fargo still held his Colt low and level. "All I did was stop them from chewing on the lady."

The dogs raised their heads to the man with the belly as if awaiting his command to attack

"It's a good thing you didn't hurt them," the tin star said. "It'd have gone hard for you, interfering with a posse." His dark eyes fixed on the Colt. They were twin points of flint, those eyes, and didn't match his pudgy body.

Since none of the three had resorted to a gun, Fargo twirled his into his holster.

"Slick," the lawman said. He glared at the woman. "I'll get to you in a minute, Carmody."

The woman mewed like a frightened kitten.

"Now, then," the pudgy man with the hard eyes said. "I'm Marshal Luther Mako. These are my deputies, Clyde and Gergan."

Fargo took an immediate dislike to both. Clyde was a rat in clothes. Gergan was skinny enough to be a rake handle. Both looked as if they wanted to take a bite out of him.

"And you might be?" Marshal Mako asked when Fargo didn't respond.

Fargo gave them his handle. He half-reckoned they might have heard of him, given the times he'd been written up in the newspapers. But they didn't act is if they had. "I scout for a living," he mentioned.

"Do you know Carmody Wells, here?" Marshal Mako asked with a bob of his fleshy chin at the terrified woman.

"I never set eyes on her before today."

"She's an escaped prisoner. She broke out of jail and—"

"Not jail!" Carmody cried. She turned to Fargo, her face twisted in appeal. "Don't listen to him. He lies with every breath. You have to help me, or I'm done for."

Marshal Mako leaned on his saddle horn and sighed.

"Broke custody, then. Does that sound better?" He looked at Fargo and sadly shook his head. "She was sentenced to six months at hard labor."

"A woman?" Fargo said.

"It's not as bad as it sounds," Marshal Mako said. "She helps with the cook wagon that goes out and feeds the work crews."

"Work crews!" Carmody said. "Men in chains, is more like it."

"Lawbreakers," Mako said. "Duly put on trial and found guilty." He motioned at the deputies. "Enough of this. Tie her up and let's head back."

Clyde and Gergan began to climb down.

Carmody Wells reached up and seized Fargo's hand. *"Please,"* she begged. "Don't let them take me. They'll whip me for sure."

Marshal Mako let out another sigh. "I've never whipped anybody, lady, and you know it." To Fargo, he said, "She was arrested for stealing and resisting arrest. She tried to stab Gergan, there. And there were witnesses."

"I didn't steal anything," Carmody said. "Honest."

The deputies walked up on either side of her.

"Come along peaceable, ma'am," Gergan said.

"We don't want to hurt you," Clyde assured her.

Carmody recoiled like a bobcat at bay. She clawed at Clyde's face, and he ducked. In a bound, she was past him, but he flung out a leg, and she tripped and fell. Before she could rise, they had her by the arms.

"Gently, boys," Marshal Mako said. "Don't hurt her if you can help it."

Fargo felt sorry for her, but he wasn't about to buck a tin star without good cause, and from the sound of things, the marshal was only doing his job.

"Come along quietly, Carmody," Mako said. "It'll be easier on you."

Carmody did no such thing. She tugged and pulled and kicked. It was all Gergan and Clyde could do to hold on to her. She landed a good kick on Clyde's shin that made him yelp, and she tried to plant her other foot between Gergan's legs.

"Calm down!" Marshal Mako commanded.

Carmody fought harder. She drove a knee into Gergan's gut, doubling him over, and she was on the verge of wrenching loose from Clyde when Marshal Mako gigged his mount and with a flick of his arm rapped her over the crown of her head with a pistol barrel.

Fargo was impressed. He'd barely seen the lawman's hand move. "Slick," he said.

Mako stared at the unconscious form on the ground. "I hated to do that. I truly did." He hefted his revolver, then shoved it into its holster. "I don't like hitting women, but she brought it on herself."

"A man does what he has to," Fargo said.

"I'm glad you see it that way." Mako ordered his deputies to bind her, then had them place her belly down over Gergan's saddle. Gergan was told to ride double with Clyde back to town.

"How about you, mister?" the lawman asked Fargo. "Care to pay Fairplay a visit?"

"Is it a dry town?"

Mako chuckled. "We have two saloons with all the liquor you could want."

"That's a lot," Fargo said.

"Then come ahead," Marshal Mako said cheerfully. "You'll find we're about the friendliest town this side of anywhere."

The woman called Carmody Wells groaned.